Off the Wall

Double-Twins Mystery #2

By: Paul Kijinski
Award-Winning Author of *Camp Limestone*

DEDICATION

*For my two favorite newlywed couples:
PJ & Sarah and Andy & Amanda*

CONTENTS

ACKNOWLEDGMENTS

Cover design by Cal Sharp at Caligraphics

The images that appear on the cover are in the public domain:

- Madonna Photograph –
  https://commons.wikimedia.org/wiki/File%3AMadonna_3_by_David_Shankbone.jpg By David Shankbone [GFDL (http://www.gnu.org/copyleft/fdl.html) or CC-BY-SA-3.0 (http://creativecommons.org/licenses/by-sa/3.0/)], via Wikimedia Commons. *Note*: The original photograph has been digitally altered to appear as a sketch on the cover.

- Tudor Style Home –
  https://commons.wikimedia.org/wiki/File%3ACompton_Gables_-_geograph.org.uk_-_856484.jpg By Colin Smith [CC BY-SA 2.0 (http://creativecommons.org/licenses/by-sa/2.0)], via Wikimedia Commons

- Map of Ohio –
  https://commons.wikimedia.org/wiki/File%3AMap_of_Ohio_NA.png

CHAPTER ONE

I felt like shaking my laptop computer—as if that would alert the Burke twins to the fact that they were already ten minutes late for our video chat. "Come on, come on," I grumbled and jabbed the mouse pointer at the AgNoDak user name.

"Give it a rest, Mark," my twin sister Mandy said with a *tsk* while turning the page of yet another mystery. "So what if they're a little late? They'll be there."

A little late didn't matter to Mandy because she had no plans that afternoon. I already had on my basketball gear for a big game at Cain Park, and my teammates would have major heart attacks if I didn't show up on time. I also didn't want my girlfriend, Sarah, to get to the park before me. She's a great girl, but she gets funny about things like that. I could just hear her saying, "It's *your* game, so why was *I* here before you?"

Finally, AgNoDak popped up online. I initiated the call and Aggie answered, appearing with a field of sunflowers behind her. That took me by surprise. I felt as though I was transported back in time to the previous summer, when my family spent a month in North Dakota in an ex-military facility that was surrounded by sunflowers.

"Whoa, where are you?" I asked.

"We're just sitting here in the apartment," Aggie assured me. Aggie was wearing a green University of North Dakota hoodie. Her brown hair, usually in a ponytail, was loose around her shoulders. She looked nice. "The sunflowers are Alex's deal," Aggie continued. "He's been messing around with CamTwist special effects."

"Boy Genius strikes again!" I laughed. Alex's pale, bespectacled face popped up behind Aggie's shoulder for a moment. He gave a thumbs-up and backed out of the camera frame again.

"So . . . how's your weather been in Ohio?" Aggie asked.

"Lots of rain, but then some pretty hot days too," I replied mechanically. "Pretty typical for May in Cleveland."

"Hmm," Aggie said with a thoughtful nod.

Here we were discussing the weather again like a couple of old fogies. Our conversations had taken a definite nosedive since Christmas, when Bobby Swenson's parents bought each of us twins a MacBook Pro. We had solved the mystery of Bobby's death, and Mr. and Mrs. Swenson insisted on buying the laptops as a way to thank us. In the beginning, our Sunday chats with the Burke twins gave us the chance to relive our exciting month together in North Dakota. Our parents had kept our names out of the news media because we're minors, and a lawyer instructed us to not discuss our role in the case with anyone, so our video chats provided a major release for us. But there's only so many times you can repeat a story without it getting stale— even when the story includes some bizarre twists and turns. Plus, things were a little awkward now between Aggie and me.

I had left North Dakota thinking of Aggie as my girlfriend, but time and distance nudged us apart. One thousand eighty-two miles separated us, to be exact, and when Sarah Beasley had one of her girlfriends tell me that she—*the* Sarah Beasley—thought I was cute, I couldn't resist the opportunity. But it's not like Aggie hadn't moved on. She even e-mailed me a photo of her and some tall kid named Rick at a school dance. Aggie looks pretty in that photo in a royal blue dress, or at least *I* think so. When I showed the picture to a few of my teammates, one of them laughed. "Dude, that's *her*?" he asked in disbelief. "From the way you were talking, I thought she'd be hot. Now I know why you dumped her for Sarah." Brandon, my best friend, had a kinder reaction: "She looks like she'd be really nice," he said sincerely, but his comment just made the other guys laugh harder. "Nice to dump so you can move on to Sarah!" one of them said. "Shut up!" I shot back angrily. "I didn't dump anybody. And Aggie's better than any girl you'll ever get."

Okay, so Aggie doesn't have the traditional cutesy look that everyone seems hooked on; she is solid, tall, and athletic. You can tell that even from the dance picture. Rick, standing next to her, is flashing a proud smile. It's a nice picture, I guess, but it makes me feel weird—kind of happy for Aggie, but sad and maybe even a little jealous at the same time.

I wondered if it was such a great idea that Aggie and Alex would be coming to visit us the following month. People change a lot in a year, especially when going from almost-twelve to almost-thirteen. I know I did. On the outside, I was taller and stronger and had to start zapping zits every now and then. On the inside, I have to admit, I became moodier and less thrilled about spending time with my family. Friends, basketball, and my girlfriend had pretty much taken over my life. "Is there anything more frightening than a teenager?" my father is fond of asking. "Um, yes. That would be teenaged twins," my mom reminds him. Very funny.

I looked at Aggie's live image on the screen and tapped my cheek. "Looks like you've been playing a lot of basketball," I observed.

"What? Oh yeah, the sunburn," Aggie laughed.

"And the extra freckles," I added.

"Yeah, yeah," Aggie said. I liked her freckles and she knew it. "Oh, you'll appreciate this," she continued and became more animated. "Craziest thing happened to me yesterday at University Park. I was warming up with free-throws before Rick and the other guys got there, and suddenly this bird swoops down and lands right on my head!"

I froze. "You've got to be kidding," I said in disbelief.

"Seriously," Aggie continued. "Landed right on my head and actually tugged at my hair until I shooshed it off with my hand. I must've looked like an idiot dancing around the basketball court!"

"The exact same thing happened to me yesterday," I announced. Tingles hadn't played up and down my spine like that since our month together in North Dakota when we were communicating with Bobby, a teenager who had met a violent death in 1964.

"Yeah, right," Aggie replied and pursed her lips. "A bird landed on your head."

"I swear to you! I was warming up, same as you, and the exact same thing happened."

Alex suddenly appeared behind Aggie again. "What kind of bird?" he asked seriously. Now even Mandy was intrigued. She rested her book on my shoulder and crouched down behind me to get in the camera frame.

"A cardinal," I responded. "But what does that matter?"

"What kind was yours?" Alex asked his sister.

"A meadowlark. So?"

"That would've been really cool if they were the same kind of bird," Mandy observed.

"In a way, they were," Alex said smugly and pushed up his glasses. I hate it when he thinks he knows everything.

"Okay, what's that supposed to mean?" I asked, annoyed.

"Do you know what Ohio's state bird is?" Alex asked.

"Of course I do," I snapped back. "It's the cardinal. I've lived here my whole life, and the last time I checked I wasn't an idiot."

"Keep checking," Mandy mumbled in my ear.

"Watch it," I warned her.

"And guess what North Dakota's state bird just happens to be?" Alex continued.

"The meadowlark?" Mandy asked hopefully.

"The western meadowlark," Alex corrected. "Which is what I'm sure my sister means when she says just *meadowlark*. And what time, exactly, did your event happen, Mark?"

"Event? If you mean the bird thing, I would have to say one-forty-five because I had a game starting at two."

"And for you, Aggie?" Alex prodded his sister.

"Twelve-forty-five because my game was at one."

"Ha!" Alex yelled and became wild eyed. "Exact same time when you take into account the difference between the Eastern and Central time zones. This is the kind of sign I've been waiting for."

"What do you mean, Alex?" Mandy asked. "What sign?"

"A sign that the four of us have more work to do," he explained. "It's like someone, or something, is telling—" Alex stopped mid-sentence and suddenly froze. He looked like a zombie.

"Now what?" I asked.

"That book," Alex said suspiciously and pointed at the camera. "What book are you reading, Mandy?"

"Oh, this?" Mandy asked. She took the book off my shoulder and held it closer to the camera. "It's called *Murder at the Ten-Pin Palace*. Some old mystery that I found at a used book store. Why?"

Alex's eyes went all fiery again and his lips trembled. *What's with this guy?* I was thinking. He looked like he was about to puke, pass out, or cry. And then he suddenly disappeared from our view.

"Now what?" I asked again in exasperation.

"I'm not sure," Aggie laughed. "You know how my brother is."

Alex reappeared and thrust his own copy of *Murder at the Ten-Pin Palace* in front of the camera. "What page are you on?" he asked hurriedly. "Come on, Mandy—what page?"

"One hundred seventy-eight," Mandy responded with eyebrows furrowed.

Alex flipped open to his bookmark. "Ha!" he cried out again. "One hundred seventy-eight, exactly! Do you have any idea what the odds are of us reading this same old book, let alone being on the same page? This is definitely another sign, people! We've got to keep our eyes open for our next assignment, because that's—"

"Whoa!" I interrupted. "Next assignment, Alex? Where are you getting this from?"

"It's our team," he said seriously. "We were able to help Bobby when we worked together, and now we're probably supposed to help someone else. We just need to look for clues as to who that is. My hunch is that since we're visiting you soon, it's probably someone in Ohio."

I started laughing; I couldn't help it. "Look, the Bobby situation was a once-in-a-lifetime thing," I said. "It was cool and I'm glad we did it, but now we move on."

"Move on to the next case," Alex insisted. "The signs are pointing that way."

"These are some weird coincidences," Mandy agreed.

"For all I know, Mandy, you and Alex planned this whole thing," I said.

"Right, Mark," Alex said sarcastically. "We planned to find the same out-of-print bowling mystery and claim we were on the same page just to mess with you. Oh, and we also placed calls to our governors and asked them to coordinate state bird attacks on you and Aggie." Alex's face had gone from pale to artery-popping red.

I had to admit, those were not everyday coincidences like bumping into a friend at the movie theater or trying to call your mom's cell phone at the exact moment she's calling yours. No, the bird and book incidents were in a league of their own. But to think that a supernatural force of some kind had arranged them was a little too creepy for me to consider at that point.

"I'd like to talk to you about this book, Mandy," Alex said. "Let's take our conversation offline."

"I'll call your cell in, like, thirty seconds," Mandy replied excitedly.

Good. I didn't want to hear what they had to say anyway. Mandy and Alex disappeared, leaving me in a face-to-face with Aggie. "Man, those sunflowers really do look real," I said lamely.

"Now that we're alone, let me ask you something," Aggie began seriously. I braced myself, thinking Aggie's question might have something to do with my relationship with Sarah, which I hadn't kept secret. "How long would it take to get from your house to Dayton?"

"Dayton?" I asked, confused. "I guess somewhere between three and four hours. Why?"

"I'll tell you more later. I've been digging around for something, and I think I might be looking for a way to get down to Dayton when we visit you."

"Well, okay. You don't want to give me any details?"

"No, not now. Sorry. And please don't say anything to Alex about this."

"Not a chance," I laughed. As if I would tell that guy anything! I glanced at the clock. "Shoot!" I exclaimed. I would need to pedal my bike like a madman in order to make it to my game on time, and I wouldn't have a moment to spare for warm-ups.

"Gotta go?" Aggie asked with a half-smile.

"Yeah, sorry."

"Take care, Mark. Have a good week."

"Okay, you too. Bye."

I closed the video chat window, grabbed a Gatorade from the fridge, and bounded out the door. Sarah would be ticked.

CHAPTER TWO

We had two more video chats with the Burke twins before the end of the school year. Alex and Mandy had selected the same CamTwist backdrop for each chat: one week it was an amusement park and the next week it was the Milky Way. These new coincidences got Alex's motor running even faster than before.

"I'm telling you guys, we're on the brink of something!" Alex exclaimed both times. "Keep your eyes open."

Whatever.

****

"Walk, young man!" that familiar voice called out in the hallway on the last day of school. It was my mother, who taught seventh-grade math. For some reason she got a kick out of giving me commands at school even when they didn't make sense. For example, I wasn't running at the time she said that; I was walking ever so slowly toward her room. Thank goodness neither Mandy nor I had her for math. She has a good reputation with kids, but it would have been too weird to have our own mom standing up in front of the classroom each day. It was bad enough that my girlfriend had her. For the last two months of school I was treated to Sarah's complaints about the amount of homework doled out by Mrs. C.—a.k.a. Mrs. Cousineau— a.k.a. my mom.

"Where's Mandy?" I asked Mom. I wanted to make sure she wasn't weaseling out of the annual task of loading our parents' cars with things they wanted to bring home for summer.

"I already sent her over to Dad's school," Mom said. "Gretchen went with her." *Great.* I could picture Mandy and her best friend lounging in Dad's fourth-grade classroom while he did all the work. He's way too easy on his precious daughter. It wouldn't have surprised me if he was serving her and Gretchen ice cold Cokes from the teachers' lounge right about then.

"Start with these, please," Mom said and pointed to a stack of file boxes. The ceiling fan whooshed lazily through the thick, muggy air, and I wasn't looking forward to carrying heavy items down a flight of stairs and out onto the sizzling parking lot. I knew there was no use in complaining, though. I would get the old question about why I seem to have so much energy for basketball, but not for the practical things my parents ask me to do.

By my fourth and final trip out of Mom's classroom, I was absolutely drenched in sweat. Plus, the two potted plants I was carrying were making me itch all over. *Mandy and Gretchen are probably sipping Cokes and reading aloud some stupid mystery,* I told myself.

"Hey, Mark!" Mr. Hoffer, my science teacher, called out from the classroom next to Mom's. The last thing I wanted to do was move some of his things too, so I pretended not to hear. But by the time I reached the top of the staircase, he was suddenly right behind me. "Mark?" he repeated, startling me.

"Whoa!" I exclaimed, losing my balance for a moment. Fortunately, I didn't drop either plant or go tumbling headlong down the stairs.

"Sorry about that," Mr. Hoffer laughed. He towered over me at six feet, three inches. He was a pretty nice forty-year-old guy, but his height, buzz-cut hair, and slightly bulging blue eyes made him intimidating to most middle school students. Myself included. "I've got a job proposal for you to consider," Mr. Hoffer said with his black licorice breath. He devoured rope after rope of Twizzlers throughout the day.

Here we go with moving stuff out to his car, I thought. And I'll probably get paid in black Twizzlers.

Mr. Hoffer stood there looking quite comfortable in a crisp shirt and tie while I sweated like crazy in my shorts and T-shirt. He didn't have any children of his own, so I figured he was planning to lean on me to do his dirty work. I hoped that my mom hadn't given him permission to do that. I pictured her offering, "When he's done with my room, he's all yours!" and my heart raced with anger. I pictured Mandy and Gretchen tipping their sweaty Coke bottles toward me in a sarcastic salute, and my blood boiled.

"If you can take a break for a second, that would be great," Mr. Hoffer said with a smile. I wondered why his teeth hadn't turned black over the years.

I set down the plants and followed him back to his room while scratching my itchy face and scalp. The familiar photo of his wife greeted us on his desktop. Mrs. Hoffer was ten years younger than her husband and surprisingly attractive, with blonde hair and light brown eyes. "She must think he's *licoricious* or something," a girl once joked in the cafeteria. Mr. Hoffer walked over to his desk and pulled out a gray lanyard, one of those cloth type necklaces that teachers wear to hold their ID badges. The lanyard had the words *Rockwell Automation* on it in red stitching, and two keys dangled from a silver ring at the end. Mr. Hoffer looked like a giant hypnotist standing before me as I watched the keys swish from left to right. *You are getting sleepy. Sleeeeepy.*

"These belonged to my Great-Aunt Arabella," Mr. Hoffer announced, dropping the lanyard on the desk and breaking my trance. "She passed away this past winter—actually, right on Christmas Day—and my sister and I are in charge of selling her house. So far we haven't received any serious offers, but hopefully our luck will turn around in the summer. Anyway, what I'm looking for is someone to mow the grass once a week, weed the flower beds, and check around inside the house. You know, to make sure nothing's leaking or burning or anything like that."

Another house-sitting gig! I thought. My family had spent an entire month house-sitting in North Dakota the previous summer. That's how Mandy and I had met the Burke twins in the first place, and how we had been drawn into the whole Bobby Swenson mystery. This summer's job wouldn't technically qualify as house-sitting, though, since I would still be living under my own roof and just visiting the old lady's house. Close enough.

"My sister Sonia may be in and out of the place from time to time as well," Mr. Hoffer continued, "but she's—how should I put this?—a little unreliable. She might start a project at the house one day, and then not come back to finish it for another two weeks. A little flighty, if you know what I mean."

"I have a sister too," I reminded Mr. Hoffer with a smile. *Okay, so how much is old Licoricious planning to pay me?* I was wondering.

Mr. Hoffer explained that his great-aunt had lived on Redwood Road, just a couple of streets away from my own street, Berkshire. My mother has been using "Redwood Road" as a tongue-twister ever since I can remember. "Say it three times real fast!" she happily demands whenever we pass the street sign. Some things just never get old as far as parents are concerned.

Mr. Hoffer said that one key on the lanyard was for the house and the other for the detached garage, where I would find the mower and any other gardening tools I might need. *Yes, and* . . . I wanted to interrupt and ask about my salary. Mr. Hoffer explained that he and his wife would be out of town a lot during the summer months and that it would put his mind at ease to know that a responsible kid was looking after the old house and keeping up its "curb appeal," by which he meant the first impression the house and yard make on prospective buyers when they pull up in front of the place. *Okay, and* . . .

And then the magic words I had been waiting to hear were finally spoken: "Oh, and I plan to pay twenty-five dollars a week—a hundred a month. Are you interested?"

"That sounds fair to me," I replied with dollar signs dancing in my head. "Thanks! I'll just need to make sure it's okay with my parents."

"I already did that. Actually, it was your mother who recommended you for the job when I mentioned it in the teachers' lounge."

I felt guilty for not being a more enthusiastic helper to my mother. I also felt a little guilty for being jealous of Mandy when I'd found out that *she* had scored a summer job the day before. She would be babysitting every Friday from 8:00 AM until noon for Mrs. Linden, the art teacher at our school. I wasn't jealous of the fact that Mandy would get to spend time with the two Linden boys, who are pretty wild and obnoxious, but I did covet her salary of twenty dollars a week. And now I came to find out that I would be making more than her after all. Not that it was a contest or anything.

"So, we have a deal then?" Mr. Hoffer asked while extending his hand. I shook it and then picked up the lanyard.

"How come it says *Rockwell Automation* on this?"

"Because that's where she worked for many years as an engineer. She was quite a character, old Aunt Arabella! Interested in so many different things. She was born in 1923 in Wooster, which, as you probably know, is a pretty rural community. But she went on to earn a degree in electrical engineering from MIT. That kind of thing was almost unheard of for a woman back in those days."

"Wow, MIT!" I exclaimed. My parents had told me that it was the best technical school in the whole country. "She must have been really smart."

"She was. And pretty strong-willed too. After her fiancé got killed during World War II, my grandfather—her brother—tried to convince her to settle down with someone else, but she wouldn't hear of it. She went out with different men over the years, but she was pretty much married to her profession and a whole slew of interests."

"Like what?"

"For one thing, she was a dedicated ornithologist." Mr. Hoffer raised his eyebrows, waiting to see if I remembered the meaning of the "o" term he had just thrown out.

"That's a bird scientist," I declared, pleased with myself.

"Hey, I guess you really were paying attention in class! Anyway, Aunt Arabella also loved astronomy, reading—mostly mysteries—and solving puzzles. Every kind of puzzle you can think of: jigsaws, crosswords, jumbles, rebuses, Magic Eyes, and then even Sudokus during the last few years of her life. Oh, and get this, she was still a roller coaster enthusiast into her late eighties! She went to Cedar Point twice every summer."

The wheels were spinning in my brain: What about the bird incidents that Aggie and I had recently experienced? What about the video chat backdrops of an amusement park and the Milky Way that Mandy and Alex had randomly selected? *Were their selections really random?* I now wondered. I remembered the novel that, mysteriously, both twins were reading. "Did she like bowling?" I asked cautiously and waited for Mr. Hoffer's response with a cringe.

"How'd you know? She was actually still on a bowling league until the day she died! I swear, if you look up the definition for *eccentric* in the dictionary, you'll find a picture of my old Aunt Arabella right next to it."

Oh boy, here we go again! I was thinking. The same electrical energy that was so familiar to me in the Foxtrot-Zero launch control center, where Bobby Swenson had lost his life, started buzzing its way up my legs again. I felt dizzy. "How did she die?" I heard myself ask.

"Do the math, as they say," Mr. Hoffer replied lightheartedly. "She was over ninety, so I think that qualifies as dying of old age, don't you? I don't remember her being ill a day in her life. She kept herself healthy and fit right until the end."

"So the end for her didn't come in a hospital?"

"No, no. Right in her home. Very peaceful. I found her in bed when I went to pick her up for our Christmas gathering." I must have had a concerned look on my face, because Mr. Hoffer added with a laugh, "That's not a problem for you that dear Aunt Arabella died in the house you'll be looking after, is it?"

"What? Oh, heck no," I assured him.

"Excellent! After all, we *are* men of science, aren't we?" Before I could answer, Mr. Hoffer took the lanyard from my hand and put it over my head. "That way you won't lose 'em," he explained and patted my shoulder.

Was I wearing the keys to a haunted house?

CHAPTER THREE

"Happy three-month anniversary!" Sarah cooed when she appeared at her screen door. She looked great, as always: shiny blonde hair, china blue eyes, and perfect teeth. Her hair was pulled back in a ponytail, showing off her golden-tanned face. Sarah has a single dimple, which rides up high on her left cheek. It's small, so you have to be close to see it, and for some reason I'm mesmerized by that thing. "Hel-*lo?*" she has said to me at times when I wasn't making good eye contact with her. Instead, I'd been gazing at the dimple.

"You'll have to wait out there for a minute because everyone's gone," she said. This meant that her mom, dad, and older brother were out at work. "I hope that's all right." *There it is!* I thought and smiled. When Sarah says *all right*, you can still hear a little Texas twang in her voice. Her family moved from Houston to Cleveland Heights when she was in second grade, but that one expression—*all right*—keeps her slightly tethered to her birthplace. That and her looks, I guess. The first day she had come over to my house for a cookout, my father took me aside and whispered, "Now you know why Miss Texas wins all the big beauty pageants. That's how they make 'em down there."

Sarah walked out into the bright noon sun and locked the door behind her. She gave me a hug and a peck on the lips and then held her hands out to the sides in a *ta-dah* pose. "Say hello to Elaine and Irene," she demanded. I knew this could mean only one thing: She had gone shopping again at Abercrombie & Fitch, where seemingly each article of clothing is christened with a proper name. I think it's a silly tradition, but I played along anyway. Elaine turned out to be a dressy tank top with a green floral pattern, and Irene was a pair of faded denim shorts—and I mean *short*—with cuffs at the bottom.

"Hello, girls," I said and tipped an imaginary hat to Elaine and Irene.

"And this, of course, is Mickey," Sarah said and pointed at her Mickey Mouse watch with pink band.

I felt majorly underdressed in khaki shorts and a brown short-sleeve polo, both of which remained nameless. "And what do you call your beaded flip-flops?" I asked.

"Comfortable!" Sarah quipped. That's the thing about Sarah: Some people, such as my sister, think she's just a Barbie doll, but then she'll go and say something clever like that. She may not be the greatest student in the world, but a B- average isn't terrible either. "Sarah should develop more of *this*," Mandy has said while tapping her head, "and less of . . . well, less of everything else." *Jealousy!* But, then again, Mandy hasn't shown any serious interest in boys yet, which is fine by me.

Sarah and I got on our bikes and began the ride down to Coventry Village, a cool neighborhood of little shops and restaurants right within Cleveland Heights. My parents call it a "hip" place to go. It was the first day of summer vacation and I was feeling stoked about the two-and-a-half month break ahead of me, especially now that I would have an income. I had decided not to say anything to Mandy about the weird conversation with my employer, Mr.

Hoffer, until I had the chance to check out the house for myself and until all four of us twins were together.

As Sarah and I approached the local CVS, we saw old Mr. Randall in his usual pose, sitting out on the store's bench in his lab coat smoking a cigarette. He must be eighty years old, and my parents say he's been a pharmacist at the same store for as long as they can remember, way before CVS took over. Mr. Randall has yellow stained fingers and teeth from smoking a decades-long chain of unfiltered cigarettes. You would think that a pharmacist would know better than to smoke. I've asked my parents why we continue going to that store. My mother's reply is, "Mr. Randall may be crotchety, but the store is so convenient." My father adds, with a laugh, "Yeah, and the old coot won't be around forever!" I gave Mr. Randall a wave and a pleasant hello, but he just stared at us as we rode by.

"Ca-*reepy*!" Sarah said when we were out of Mr. Randall's earshot.

We eventually locked our bikes outside a restaurant called Tommy's, where they serve the best sandwiches and malted milkshakes on the planet. Sarah was looking fresh as a daisy, but my shirt was sporting a few quarter-sized sweat marks. The college-aged hostess walked us along a lunch counter and sat us at a wooden booth. Just like Sarah's clothing, the sandwiches at Tommy's have names. Sarah was at first thinking that she owed it to Elaine, her top, to order an Elaine, a flipsteak sandwich, but then she was afraid that the one Elaine might drip BBQ sauce on the other. We both finally settled on a K.S., which is a grilled ham and Swiss cheese sandwich served on pita bread. We would share a basket of homemade fries and a large chocolate malt.

"I love how they bring you the tin cup and then just leave it at your table," I said. Sarah smiled, revealing her dimple.

My sister's favorite feature of Tommy's is its connection to Mac's Backs, a bookstore with three floors of new and used titles. That's where she bought her copy of the bowling mystery. When we come to Tommy's with our parents, Mandy instructs "Daddy" what to order for her, and then she disappears through the Mac's Backs portal until our food is on the table. The only thing that would get Sarah into Mac's, though, would be the magazine rack. She has a thing for *Seventeen Magazine*, even though she's only thirteen, and for *Us Weekly*.

"I've been thinking," Sarah began. "Isn't it gonna be a little awkward when your friends from North Dakota are here? I mean, I know you kind of liked that girl."

That was all Sarah knew about my relationship with Aggie. I hadn't told her, or anyone else, about the unique connection I had forged with Aggie through the whole Bobby Swenson ordeal. The only people that Mandy and I had confided in were our parents, and even they had a hard time believing us. Dad's response went like this: "It could be that you kids were just seeing what you wanted to see. That launch control center is kind of like one of those sensory deprivation chambers. Let's face it: it's flat-out boring down there. And when the mind doesn't receive any interesting stimuli from outside, it tends to make up its own." Mom chimed in with her theory that since twins are so often on the same wavelength, it would be easy for us to experience a kind of "mass delusion." I didn't see how this could apply to *two sets* of *fraternal* twins, but I didn't argue with her. The bottom line was that we were sworn to secrecy about anything supernatural that we "believed" we had experienced. *Believed* we had experienced? We knew better.

"I think it'll be fine," I assured Sarah. "You'll get along okay with both of the Burkes, and it's only for a week."

The twins would stay with us while Ms. Burke and her two brothers fixed up a house she had just bought in Grand Forks. Ms. Burke had been the superintendent of Squires Hall, a dormitory at University of North Dakota, which meant that she and twins actually lived in a dormitory apartment. Now that she had finished her degree in accounting and found a new job, though, the family would be moving into a standalone house. My parents were kind enough to buy the twins airline tickets with points they'd earned on their credit card. "That'll keep them out of your hair while you paint," my mother had said to Ms. Burke on the phone. "Plus, we'd all love to see them again."

When our food arrived, Sarah reached across the table and took my hand. "Happy anniversary," she said.

"Happy anniversary," I repeated. I knew that a so-called three-month anniversary really didn't make any sense, but I kept my mouth shut and just smiled. What did I have to complain about? It was summer vacation and I was holding hands with the prettiest girl at Roxboro Middle School.

As we ate, Sarah told me about an article she had read in *Us Weekly* about pickup lines used around the world. "My favorite one comes from Japan, and it goes, 'I hope that a year from now we'll be laughing together.' That's so romantic, isn't it?"

"Mm-hm," I grunted while savoring my K.S. sandwich. I thought the line was lame, actually. A pickup line is used when you're just meeting someone. So, would it really make sense to go up to a girl you've never met before and say, "Hi, it's nice to meet you. Oh, and by the way, I hope that a year from now we'll be laughing together"? Maybe it sounds better in Japanese.

"So . . ." Sarah began.

"So what?"

"Do you think that a year from now *we'll* be laughing together?" she asked.

"Absolutely!" I replied confidently and took a long sip of chocolate malt.

"Well, all right!" Sarah twanged.

CHAPTER FOUR

There's an expression that goes, "Look before you leap." I should have kept that in mind when I agreed to take care of Ms. Arabella Hoffer's place. She turned out to have a corner lot with an average sized front yard, but a humongous backyard that would take forever to mow. Maybe twenty-five dollars a week wasn't such a great deal after all. I was hoping I had the wrong address, but it was the only house on that side of the street with a realty sign planted in front of it. At least the two flowerbeds were narrow, so weeding them wouldn't be hard to keep up with. And the hedges had been recently trimmed, so I assumed they weren't my responsibility. Mr. Hoffer had never said anything about hedges.

The house itself was one of the smallest on the street and was built in the Tudor style, which my mother loves. A Tudor is easy to spot because it has timber beams that criss-cross the front of the house in a pattern. Bricks, stones, or plaster fills the spaces in between. The beams on Ms. Hoffer's place were stained dark brown and the plaster was the color of French vanilla ice cream. A tall stone chimney told me there would be a fireplace inside. The house looked pretty cozy, like a cottage or a bed-and-breakfast inn.

The detached garage housed only lawn and garden equipment. If Ms. Hoffer was still a driver when she died, her car must have gone to a family member. The Bolens lawnmower appeared to be only a season or two old, and I was glad to see the words *Super Mulching Mower*, which meant that I wouldn't have to bag the grass clippings. I topped off the gas tank, pressed the primer button a few times, and started the engine with a single pull. Not bad! At my house I have to do battle with an ancient mower that my father refuses to replace. "Well, maybe next year," he says sincerely every spring. Meanwhile, I wind up spending almost as much time starting the mower as I do cutting the lawn.

It took me about two hours to cut Ms. Hoffer's front and back lawns and weed her flowerbeds. That included time for a couple of Gatorade breaks. It was just after noon when I locked my Bolens buddy in the garage and walked to the front of the house. I opened the screen door and found a metal combination box dangling from the knob of the main door. I knew what that was: The box held a house key for real estate agents to use when showing the place to buyers. Agents need to be really trustworthy people, I guess, because they can get the combos for any house on the market.

I inserted the key that Mr. Hoffer had given me and then stopped for a moment. The whole time I was doing yard work, I kept telling myself, "It'll be no big deal to go in her house. So what if she died here? You're the guy who played chess last summer with a kid who died in 1964!" Now, with Ms. Hoffer's living space—and dying space—just a knob-turn away, I wasn't feeling so confident anymore. I got creeped out all over again about the coincidences Mandy and I had experienced with the Burke twins, coincidences that seemed to be pushing us toward this very location. But why?

I decided to take the band-aid removal approach: The faster you rip, the less it hurts. I counted in a whisper to three and then . . . jerked the knob to the right and pushed my way into the living room. Nothing greeted me except for musty heat. All of the windows were closed, and if the place had air conditioning, it definitely hadn't kicked on for some time. The furniture pieces in the living room must have been antiques. There were two wingback chairs with fancy carving on the wooden arms and legs, and a long sofa—also perched on wooden legs—to match. The upholstery featured pink and red roses. I opened out the doors of a large cabinet and found a twenty-five inch television, a DVD player, and a Bose Wave music system along with a shelf full of CDs, mostly jazz and classical. Ms. Hoffer had only a handful of DVDs. The one that caught my attention was a homemade disc titled *Our Lady Is 80!* with a picture of birthday balloons on the front of the case. On the back it read *A Jonas Hoffer Production.* I knew that my science teacher's first name was Jonas, so I figured that this was a highlights DVD he'd made on the occasion of his great-aunt's eightieth birthday. I slid the disc back into its position and closed the cabinet doors.

The coffee table had sturdy carved legs and a white marble top. The lamps on the matching end tables looked like red-tinged vases with gold leaves and crystal flowers cropping out of them. There was also a floor lamp with a cloth shade like a fringed umbrella. Books were everywhere—on built-in shelves, on standalone shelves, on the coffee table, and even on the mantelpiece. Hanging above the mantel was an old color photograph of a young woman with a soldier. They were standing arm in arm in front of an ivy-covered building. I figured that it must be Ms. Hoffer and her fiancé. "Madonna!" I whispered, because that's exactly who Ms. Hoffer looked like—the singer Madonna. She had the same blonde hair, same sparkling blue eyes, same mischievous smile, and even the same little space between her front teeth.

The living room had a cluttered, cozy feel to it. I felt pretty comfortable. I picked up the receiver of an ivory and gold-colored telephone that looked like an antique, except that it had push buttons instead of a rotary dial. The line was dead, which made sense: Why pay for phone service when no one is there to use it?

I walked through the elegant dining room and into the kitchen, which had a black-and-white tile floor. Three of the walls were painted white, but the fourth was covered from floor to ceiling in wallpaper that my mother would call *hideous* or *garish*. It had splotches of many different colors—greens, blues, reds, yellows, browns—and no particular pattern that I could make out. I stared at it for a while and actually got a little lightheaded, the way I do when trying to solve Magic Eye puzzles. Mandy can always find the hidden 3-D images right away, but I've never once been successful. I've faked it a few times, saying, "Oh, sweet! Look at that!" But Mandy baits me, "Prove it. What, exactly, do you see?" And, of course, I fail her test. She thinks it's hysterical that I'm Magic Eye-challenged. She has even suggested to my parents that they find a special Magic Eye camp for me to attend on the weekends.

A small breakfast table sat in front of a stained glass window in Ms. Hoffer's kitchen, and I imagined colorful light streaming through it in the morning. Right next to the window was a door that led out to a small cobblestone patio. A bowling trophy caught my attention from across the room, standing tall among knick-knacks on a shelf above the sink. I picked it up and read the inscription: *Top Score, Senior Division: 178*. "Wow!" I said aloud. That was really an impressive score, especially for such an old woman. And then I suddenly flashed back to the fateful video chat with the Burke twins. I was nearly positive that Mandy and Alex had said they were both on page 178 of the *Ten-Pin Palace* mystery, and now there I was holding a bowling trophy with that same number on it! I quickly returned the award to its place on the shelf. My mind was racing. *What's the connection? If we're being drawn here for some reason, what is it?*

Just then, a vibration in my pocket made me jump and bash my hip against the counter. "Phone!" I said aloud. I pulled out my cell and saw that Mandy was calling. "What?" I answered angrily while rubbing my side.

"These kids are driving me nuts," Mandy moaned. She was babysitting the Lindens.

"Why are you still there?"

"Mrs. Linden called to say she's running late. I'll be here for at least another hour. Look, is there any chance you can stop by and shoot baskets or something with these guys?"

"I'm pretty tired from doing yard work. Why don't you get Gretchen to help you?"

"Gretchen left for Myrtle Beach today. Come on, Mark. I'll pay you five dollars." She was exasperated.

"I'm on my way. One quick question, though. What's that book about—you know, the bowling mystery that you and Alex read?"

"Why? What does that have to do with anything?"

"The sooner you tell me, the sooner I'll be over there."

Mandy sighed and then rushed through a synopsis: "The manager of a bowling alley is found shot dead; there are several suspects because lots of people hated the guy; turns out the assistant manager's wife did it so her husband could get the top job. The end."

"Any old ladies involved?" I asked. "Like in their eighties?"

"Negative. Now, please get over here."

Mandy's call for help gave me an excuse to get out of Ms. Hoffer's place. I was feeling too antsy to do a complete walkthrough anyway, so I just stood there in the kitchen for a moment and verified that I didn't hear water running. All clear. I also opened an accordion door leading to the basement and poked my head in to sniff for a natural gas leak. Nothing except for the smell of paint.

I nodded my head like a proud homeowner and set out to rescue my sister. The combination box jangled as I slammed the door shut behind me.

CHAPTER FIVE

"We're back in business," Alex declared with a wry smile. It was Monday evening and the four of us twins were sitting out on the deck after dinner. I had just finished telling them everything I'd discovered at Ms. Hoffer's place.

"You're right," Mandy said. "All the signs are pointing to a call for help."

The Burkes had arrived from North Dakota that afternoon, and our reunion at Hopkins Airport wasn't as awkward as I thought it might be. I hugged Aggie and shook Alex's hand while giving him a guy-slap on the back. Alex annoys me when he plays Mr. Know-It-All, but I had no hard feelings toward him at the moment; it was just really nice to be all together again, face to face. I couldn't help noticing that Alex was more fit than he had been the previous summer—not quite as skinny or pale. I had shot up in height the most, though, now just an inch shy of Aggie. She looked the same: sparkly brown eyes and sun-streaked brown hair pulled back in a ponytail. It was great to be with her again.

"Why would Ms. Hoffer need anyone's help?" I asked. "With Bobby it was obvious because he was murdered. But when somebody dies of old age at home, what's the big deal? Sorry if that sounds mean, but you know what I'm saying."

"Maybe she still had some unfinished business," Aggie observed. "Even at ninety-two years old, there might have been something important that she kept putting off."

"Or, like Mr. Hoffer told you, she really loved puzzles and mysteries," Mandy reminded us. "Maybe this is her way of pulling us into a kind of puzzle of her own. She might just be looking to have a little fun with us."

"Or, maybe she was murdered," Alex offered matter-of-factly. The *m*-word cut through the humid air like a knife. "We shouldn't rule that out just because she was so old."

"Why would someone want to kill her?" Aggie asked.

"Most likely one or more of the big three reasons," Alex replied and paused. He counted on his fingers: "Anger, jealousy, or greed."

"Even if that were true, what would cause her to get us involved?" I asked. "She never even met any of us."

"Bobby!" Mandy exclaimed as though he'd just sneaked up behind us on the deck. I actually looked over my shoulder.

"What about him?" I asked.

"Well, maybe he somehow made contact with Ms. Hoffer and told her we can be helpful with . . . you know, this kind of thing," Mandy explained.

I could picture Bobby handing out business cards in heaven: *Double-Twins Mystery Services*. He would give us his personal endorsement, like my father does when recommending the plumber he's used for over twenty years. I smiled at the thought of Bobby trying to drum up business for us, but then I swallowed nervously. Was it really a laughing matter if we had become the topic of dead people's conversations?

"Mandy's theory is quite plausible," Alex concluded with a slow nod. Some of my old resentment toward Boy

Genius began to resurface. I mean, what kind of thirteen-year-old uses the expression *quite plausible*?

"Before we come up with any more theories, why don't we go over to the house and have a look around?" Aggie suggested. We all agreed that was a sensible plan.

It was only seven-thirty and there would be daylight until close to nine, so my parents had no problem with us heading out. Mandy and I said we would be showing the Burkes around the neighborhood, which was true, but we didn't specifically mention going to Ms. Hoffer's house. My parents would have been suspicious. I stuck the lanyard and keys in a cargo pocket, and off we went.

"It's so cute!" Aggie proclaimed when we stood facing the Tudor style home. "What a handsome house!" she had said that afternoon when we arrived at our red brick colonial from the airport. I had never heard our house called *handsome* before, but once she'd said it, I realized that it does have a solid, masculine appearance. By contrast, Ms. Hoffer's place was *cute*.

My fellow twins loved how old-fashioned everything looked in the living room. "You don't find many settees these days," Alex said and ran his hand along the top of the long sofa.

"Settee?" I repeated.

"That's what you call this bench-style sofa," he explained.

"Oh, yeah," I said with a nod. *Why does he know these things?* I wondered.

Mandy pulled a Magic Eye book from the mantelpiece and set it on the coffee table. "Come on," she said. "Let's flip to a page and see who can find the hidden picture first. I'm betting it won't be Mark."

"Very funny," I responded. "Hysterical." I didn't even waste my time looking with the rest of them.

"Got it!" Alex announced first, naturally, and the girls simultaneously repeated those words a moment later.

"Your call," Mandy said to Alex.

"A seal balancing a ball on his nose," he replied while tapping his own nose. *Big deal.*

They did another picture challenge and I was thrilled that Aggie beat her brother this time. "Balloons floating up in the sky," she said.

"*Helium* balloons," Alex corrected.

"What other kind of balloons float, you jerk?" Aggie asked.

I laughed. "Hey, if you guys feel up to it, let's see how you do with the granddaddy of all Magic Eye puzzles." I was messing with them, of course, just to see if they were gullible enough to stare at the kitchen wallpaper. They looked at me through narrowed eyes for an explanation. "Follow me," I said importantly. I led them into the next room and just pointed at the wall.

"Whoa!" they gasped. *Suckers!*

After a minute of nearly touching the wall with their noses, squinting, and moving back several paces to stare, Mandy suddenly cried out, "I got it!"

I quietly chuckled.

"Don't say, don't say!" Alex pleaded. And, sure enough, about fifteen seconds later, he and Aggie also hollered, "Got it!"

Okay, so now they were messing with *me*. "Yeah, right," I said, determined to not play the fool. I looked around the kitchen and spotted a pad of sticky notes and a cup of pencils on the counter. I slapped down a sticky in three different locations and handed each twin a pencil. "Write down what you claim to see," I demanded.

They were happy to oblige. I watched them like a hawk, like a teacher watches his students while they're taking the state achievement tests. No possibility of cheating. The girls were done writing almost immediately, but Alex scribbled on. "Time," I finally announced. "Pencils down." I walked from one test-taker to the next, pulling up sticky notes and collecting pencils.

Coins, Mandy's sticky read.

Old coins, Aggie's read.

Liberty Double-Eagle gold coins ($20 denomination) and Morgan silver dollars, Alex's read.

I was shocked. I followed the same steps the other twins had followed—getting close to the wall, squinting, backing away, crossing my eyes—but nothing worked. I had been annoyed about being Magic Eye-challenged in the past, but now I was really angry. I was the hired caretaker for Ms. Hoffer's place, and it didn't seem fair that I was the only one who couldn't see the image.

"You know, being able to see autostereograms really isn't a major test of intelligence or anything, so don't worry about it," Alex said in a sincere attempt to console me. Instead, I was ticked that he knew the technical name for Magic Eye puzzles.

"You wanna go one-on-one right now at the basketball court?" I blurted out in response.

"Um, yeah," Alex said sarcastically. "That'll help us figure out what's going on here."

The girls laughed, and I felt my face get hot. I knew that what I had said was stupid, but I couldn't help myself. "Okay, so what about the coins," I asked. "Why would somebody buy wallpaper with an auto . . ." I paused, trying desperately to remember the word Alex had used.

"Autostereogram," he prompted.

"I know," I assured him. "Why would somebody buy wallpaper with an autostereogram of coins hidden in it?"

"She must have been a collector," Alex said.

"And because she liked puzzles so much, maybe she paid a designer to make her this custom wallpaper," Aggie added.

What they were saying sounded reasonable to me when I considered how quirky Ms. Hoffer had been. As Mr. Hoffer had told me, his Great-Aunt Arabella's picture should appear in the dictionary beside the word *eccentric*.

I took charge again and led the group down to a completely bare basement, with the exception of a washer and dryer. The walls and floor were dry but freshly painted, just as my nose had detected the other day. We then went up to the second floor where we found a bathroom, a bedroom, and a den. The bathroom was small and had one of those old-fashioned tubs that aren't attached to the wall. Instead, it sat up on claw feet. The bedroom reminded me of pictures my mom had taken when she and my dad stayed at an inn for their anniversary. They had been down in Holmes County, also known as Amish Country because of all the Amish families who still live there. Anyway, my mom had been thrilled with the room's solid cherry furniture, especially the rice bed with four high posts.

"Check it out—a rice bed," I observed. "Most likely Amish made." *Take that, Alex!*

"Why do they call it a rice bed?" Aggie asked.

"See here in the middle of the posts? They carve rice plants," I explained while running my fingers over the handiwork. "It's a sign of God's blessing." Both Aggie and Alex nodded their heads, looking sufficiently impressed. Fortunately, Mandy didn't rat me out and say that I was just parroting what we had heard our mother say so many times.

On the nightstand was another picture of Ms. Hoffer with the same young man, only this time he wasn't in uniform. They were both in swimsuits at a beach, happy again, and he was holding her like a groom about to carry his bride over the threshold. Family photos were on the wall, including one in which I spotted a very young Jonas Hoffer, my science teacher, making rabbit ears behind his sister's head. My favorite photo, though, was of Ms. Hoffer seated before a cake with two number candles—a 9 and a 0—perched on top. Her hair is snow-white in the picture, making her blue eyes all the more striking, and she has a smile that is full of life and mischief. I felt like copying that picture and sending it to Madonna along with a note: *Dearest M – This is what you'll look like in several decades.* The picture reminded me of the *Our Lady Is 80!* DVD that Mr. Hoffer had made. I told the other twins about it, and they all agreed we should borrow it on our way out.

The bedroom was very tidy, but the den was cluttered, especially Ms. Hoffer's desk. Stacks of books stood like shaky towers on either side of her MacBook laptop, a slightly older model of the computer that we twins had.

"We could have videochatted with her if we had known about her," I joked.

A colorful poster of state birds took up most of one wall. "Hey, Aggie," I said and pointed at the poster. And then I grabbed a fistful of my hair to remind her of our experience with the cardinal and the western meadowlark. "Oh yeah!" she exclaimed. There was also a poster of the solar system and an 8" x 10" photo of Ms. Hoffer in cap and gown on her graduation day from MIT. She is standing between two dashing men in their fifties, the older of the two wearing a cap and gown, and the younger in a three-piece suit. *To Arabella, one of Wooster's finest . . .* reads the inscription in black ink, along with each man's autograph: *Karl Compton* and *Arthur Compton.*

"These guys look pretty important," Mandy observed.

"Let's see who they are," Alex said. He flipped open the laptop and took it out of the sleep mode.

"The phone service has been cut," I informed him. "So I doubt that she still has an Internet hookup."

"We'll sniff for a Wi-Fi connection," Alex replied, pushing up his glasses. Sure enough, someone in the neighborhood was pumping out a strong enough signal for us to share. Alex discovered on Wikipedia that the Compton brothers were born in Wooster, Ohio, just like Ms. Hoffer. They were much older than her, though, born in 1887 and 1892. Karl went on to become the president of MIT, which explains why he appears in cap and gown in the photo: As president, he would have been handing out diplomas that day. Arthur, his younger brother, actually won the Nobel Prize for physics in 1927. We were all impressed—especially Alex, who said he would do more research on the Compton Effect, for which Arthur had won the prize.

"Wow!" Aggie exclaimed. "Aunt Arabella really kept some serious company." I liked that Aggie had said *Aunt Arabella* instead of *Ms. Hoffer*. It made her seem more friendly and approachable, like a family member. From that moment on, that's how all of us twins referred to her.

We sorted through Aunt Arabella's books—books on birdwatching, on the universe, on various types of puzzles, on amusement parks, on bowling, and on world history. She also had several manuals from Rockwell Automation that explained the hardware and software products the company made to run factory machines.

"You know what's weird is that I don't see any books on coin collecting," Mandy remarked. That was a good observation. If Aunt Arabella had been so interested in coins, as her strange wallpaper had led us to believe, then why wouldn't she have any books on the subject?

Alex picked up an ivory-handled pocketknife from the desk. "Have you ever been to Saint Michael's Lanes on Union Avenue?" he asked. "That's what it says on this knife."

"No, never heard of it," I replied. "Union is in a pretty rundown neighborhood, though. No way my dad would take us there." Alex handed me the knife, which featured a corkscrew and bottle opener in addition to a three-inch blade. The phone number for the bowling alley was printed as DI1-9541. I knew the knife must be really old because people haven't used letters at the beginning of phone numbers for around forty years. I once found a personal phone book that my father had created when he was just a kid. The phone numbers of his friends and relatives all started with two letters, like MI, DI, and BR. My dad explained to me that someone at the phone company had thought it would be easier for people to remember phone numbers if they began with words like MIchigan, DIamond, and BRoadway. He said his own number as a kid started with MOntrose, which worked out to 66 on the phone's dial or, later, keypad. Anyway, the knife must have been decades old.

Alex Googled *St. Michael's Lanes in Cleveland* and the phone number itself, but came up with no match for either one. He keyed in the address and found that it now belonged to a business called Luke's Carpet Warehouse & Cleaning. Luke's website said that his family had been proudly serving Northeast Ohio from the same location since 1965, which meant that St. Michael's Lanes had been gone that long. We were curious about why Aunt Arabella would have kept the knife out on her desk after all these years. "Unless she just got in the habit of using the blade as a letter opener," Aggie reasoned.

Mandy's phone rang; it was our mom reminding us to come home. Alex closed the laptop and we headed downstairs. I stood in the kitchen for a moment, staring at the infamous wallpaper one more time. Aggie stayed behind with me while Alex and Mandy headed into the living room. Aggie put a hand on my back and walked me up to the wall.

"Just relax," she advised. "And pretend you're going into a trance." My vision went a little blurry and I didn't fight it. "Okay, now let's move together," Aggie whispered. She gently guided me backwards four steps.

I never took my eyes off the wall and I didn't fight the blurriness. And then, suddenly—like smoke puffed through a screen—the picture appeared before me with a 3-D depth that was beyond belief. Only it wasn't coins that I saw; it was a skull and crossbones! The eyes and nasal cavity were black, but the teeth were bright white and clenched in a hideous smile.

"Oh my goodness!" Aggie exclaimed, and I knew that she was seeing it too.

"Come on, guys!" Mandy called out from the living room.

"You need to come in here," Aggie responded mechanically while the two of us kept our eyes glued to the wall. "Look again," Aggie whispered when our twins reentered the kitchen.

"How the . . .?" Mandy began.

"Oh, man!" Alex mumbled a couple of times and laughed to himself like a lunatic. "Now this is really getting good. Aunt Arabella is trying to tell us something new."

I angled my eyes away from the wall and observed the amazed expressions on the other twins' faces. "Skull and crossbones?" I asked with a shiver, and they all gently nodded their heads.

"Like on the flag of a pirate ship," Mandy said.

"Or on a bottle of poison," Aggie added.

"That's it!" Alex shouted, breaking the spell. Everyone looked away from the wall. "Someone poisoned her!"

"Why?" I asked. "Who would want to do that?"

"Let's ask her," Mandy said and looked at the wallpaper again. "If someone poisoned you, Aunt Arabella, who was it?"

The four of us stepped close to the wall, and I wondered if everyone else was as unsteady as I was. Nervous energy tingled in my legs and shoulder blades. "Who's in there?" an old woman's gravelly voice suddenly called out. We all jumped, bumping into one another.

The voice had come from the direction of the living room, thank goodness, and not from the wallpaper. I looked to my fellow twins, who were all as wide-eyed as I must have been. None of them appeared interested in leading the way out of the kitchen.

"I'm about to call the police," the voice warned. "So you'd better show yourselves. Now!"

Mr. Hoffer had put me in charge of his great-aunt's house, so I took a deep breath and barged into the living room with the other twins close behind. Pressed up against the screen door, between two hands, was the wrinkled face of a gray-haired African American woman. Her lips were twisted in a sneer, and it looked as if she was auditioning for a role at one of those Halloween haunted houses.

"Whoa!" I exclaimed and halted the parade of twins.

"Are you the grass-cutting boy?" she asked, staring at me.

"Yes, ma'am," I replied. "That's me."

She pulled her face away from the screen and relaxed her expression. She opened the door and took a step in. She was in her eighties and petite, shorter than any of us twins.

"I recognize you from when you worked in the yard last Friday," she explained. Her voice was still raspy, but her tone was a lot friendlier. "I'm Mrs. Fields from next door. I just wanted to make sure no one was stealing from my old friend, Arabella."

"You knew her a long time?" Mandy asked.

"Lived side by side with her for forty-three years," Mrs. Fields said with pride. "Arabella was like a big sister to me." And then she turned to me. "Now, young man, what are you doing here in the evening? You're not planning to host parties in this house, are you?"

"No, definitely not," I assured her and explained who my guests were.

"That's just darling!" she exclaimed. "Boy-girl twins like the Bobbseys. And two sets at that! Mm-mm-mm." Mrs. Fields may have been small, but she had a firm grip when she shook all of our hands. She said she had three grown grandchildren and a great-granddaughter who was about our age.

Mandy's phone rang again. "Excuse me," she said to Mrs. Fields and stepped deeper into the living room to answer. "No, Mom, of course we're not lost," we heard Mandy say. "We'll be there in five minutes. I promise."

"Sounds like you kids better be on your way," Mrs. Fields advised. We all stepped out onto the front porch.

"Just a sec," I said. "I forgot to check one thing." I went directly to the TV cabinet to retrieve the *Our Lady Is 80!* DVD and stuck it in my cargo pocket so Mrs. Fields wouldn't see. I returned to where the others were waiting and locked the door.

On her way down the steps, Mrs. Fields picked up a metal cane that was leaning against a bush. "This was my husband's before he passed away," she explained. "I don't need it for walking," she laughed, "but it sure would have come in handy if I had to bash in someone's head over here!" She lifted the cane high in the air and brought it down with great force on an imaginary skull. Her hoarse laughter rattled out into a fit of coughing, but that didn't stop her from bashing. She must have caved in a dozen skulls as she cut across Aunt Arabella's front lawn.

The four of us twins looked at each other with mouths half-open. I was confident that the others shared my impression of Mrs. Fields: She was either a fun-loving great grandma with loads of energy, or she was straight-up crazy.

CHAPTER SIX

My parents took us to IHOP the next morning for breakfast. Dad drove separately so he could go directly to work at the Home Depot afterward. He had left the house the same time as us, but he arrived at the restaurant almost ten minutes later.

"OCD kick in?" Mom asked playfully without looking up from her menu. Dad just rolled his eyes, but he didn't deny the charge regarding Obsessive-Compulsive Disorder. He doesn't have a full-blown case of it, but he has been known to race back home to make sure doors are locked or to verify that the oven is off. The worst incident occurred one day when we had just arrived at Wildwater Kingdom, at least twenty miles from our home, and Dad sent us into the park while he zipped home to "check on things."

I normally savor my Belgian waffle and bacon at IHOP, but I was preoccupied with the idea of getting back to Aunt Arabella's house as soon as possible. Based on the lack of conversation among us twins, I supposed we were all on the same page. Aunt Arabella seemed like a regular family member to us now that we'd watched the DVD Mr. Hoffer made. *Our Lady Is 80!* opens with a shot of a "Welcome to Wooster" sign. Then upbeat classical music begins playing in the background while old photos fade in and out. Arabella grows up before our very eyes: she bites her own baby toes; mooshes her face against a Springer Spaniel's;

receives her First Holy Communion dressed like a little bride; pulls a younger boy in a wagon; plays badminton on a huge lawn; throws her arms around the necks of two girlfriends; pops up along the edge of a swimming pool wearing a tight bathing cap; wins a science fair award; and goes to prom with the skinniest, tallest boy you could imagine. A grainy home movie clip shows her on the campus of the College of Wooster, giving a tour to a group of prospective students and their parents. When Arabella gets right in front of the camera, she playfully sticks out her tongue. Other clips show her receiving her diploma from Karl Compton at MIT and dancing with her soldier fiancé. Eventually, video clips with sound take over. Aunt Arabella takes a dramatic bow after bowling a strike. She is onstage at a huge convention sharing her vision for "the future of industrial automation." She is in the front car of Cedar Point's Blue Streak roller coaster with a friend, their hands raised defiantly as the train begins its chain-clinking ascent. She is at family gatherings for birthdays and graduations and Christmases, getting slightly older every few seconds, but still full of life. Her voice is crisp and energetic, especially when she talks to kids. "Are you sure you're only seven years old?" she asks a beaming birthday boy. "With that wonderful brain of yours and those strong muscles, I thought for sure you were at least twelve!" Aunt Arabella's laughter is sometimes hearty and other times quiet, like she's sharing a mischievous plot with you, and only you.

"Jeez, where's the funeral?" my father asked while scooting a piece of sausage through syrup. "If anyone has the right to be mopey, I think that would be me." He put the sausage in his mouth and pointed dramatically at the nametag on his Home Depot shirt. It would be his first day back to his usual summer job after taking a break the previous summer to work on a novel. He never let Mandy or me read his manuscript because parts of it were supposedly inappropriate for kids, but my mom thought it was great. She had decided to serve as Dad's "literary agent" during the summer, trying to sell his masterpiece to publishing houses.

"Hey, Mr. C.," Aggie began. "I know you used to be in the Air Force. Somebody back in Grand Forks was telling me about a big Air Force museum you guys have here in Ohio. In Dayton, I think?"

I felt terrible because I had forgotten about Aggie's mysterious desire to visit Dayton. But, it looked like she had figured out an angle all on her own for getting my father to take us there.

"Wright-Patt!" Dad replied happily. "The official National Museum of the Air Force is there at Wright-Patterson Air Force Base. I haven't been there in years—not since the twins were in strollers."

"Would it take long to get there?" Aggie asked.

"Just three and a half hours or so," Dad said, and I could tell from the dazzled look in his eyes that he was already there among the Air Force artifacts. "We could make it a day trip on Thursday if you guys are interested. I have the day off."

"That would be great!" Aggie said and looked at me.

"Yeah, Dad. That would be cool," I agreed. I finally put two and two together and figured that the trip to Dayton must have something to do with Aggie's father. She had told me last summer that he was a sergeant in the Air Force and that he had left the family when the twins were just little kids. Maybe he was stationed at Wright-Patterson.

"Thursday's the day we're heading to the Great Lakes Science Center for the Einstein exhibit," Mom reminded us.

"Shoot!" Dad exclaimed. "Well, Aggie, maybe next time you guys visit, we can—"

"I'd take the Dayton trip over Einstein," I interrupted him. Aggie smiled at me.

It was decided that Mandy and Alex would go with my mom to the Science Center, while Aggie and I would go with my dad to the Air Force Museum. Alex was torn because of his interest in historical aircraft, but in the end he couldn't say no to his old buddy Albert E.

"*Our* museum is free," Dad boasted. "So we'll take the money we're saving on entrance tickets and slap that right in the PT Cruiser's gas tank." He was in a great mood when we went our separate ways in the parking lot.

By the time we got home and started walking over to Aunt Arabella's, it was already eleven-fifteen and pretty warm in the sun. I took the lanyard off my neck when we reached Redwood Road, but we all stopped in our tracks when we saw a white Cadillac Escalade parked in Aunt Arabella's driveway. We walked closer and noticed that the front door to the house was already open. A Taylor Swift song floated through the screens.

"Maybe Mrs. Fields drives an Escalade and jams to Taylor Swift," I said in jest. Then I looked to the neighboring yard and saw Mrs. Fields sitting on her front porch glider, staring at us. I gave a friendly wave, hoping that she hadn't heard my remark. She tossed back a salute.

"What do we do?" Mandy asked through a fake smile.

"Maybe it's a real estate agent," Alex reasoned. "Let's go check. I mean, Mr. Hoffer hired Mark to take care of the place, so it's not like we're trespassers."

"Hello?" I called through the screen door, feeling like I was reenacting Mrs. Field's visit from the previous night. "Hello?" I repeated a little louder.

A woman in her thirties suddenly appeared from the kitchen wearing white overalls and a painter's cap with wisps of platinum-blonde hair escaping here and there. She had smudges of hunter green paint on the overalls, but she looked more like a model pretending to be a painter than an actual painter. She was that pretty.

"May I help you?" she asked and dabbed perspiration from her forehead with a handkerchief. As my dad likes to say, "A man sweats, but a lady perspires."

"Um, hi," I started awkwardly. She was *really* pretty. "I'm Mark Cousineau, and my science teacher, Mr. Hoffer, hired me to take care of this yard and make sure everything is okay inside the house."

"Everything's okay," she said cheerfully. "Your science teacher is my brother. I'm Sonia. Come on in."

"Thanks, Ms. Hoffer," I said and led the way in. The other twins followed.

"It's Jenkins, actually," she said. "I keep meaning to change it back to Hoffer seeing as how I've been divorced for over a year now. Time flies. Whatever. Anyway, just call me Sonia. I'd shake your hands, but—" She finished her explanation by showing us paint-stained hands. "I'm not the handiest person in the world, but I figure I should at least look the part. These bib overalls are official Dickies. Aren't they darling?"

This last comment was directed at the girls, and they nodded in agreement. I immediately thought of Sarah, who would have been much more enthusiastic about the darlingness of Sonia's bib overalls. In fact, if Sarah were suddenly forced to paint, her first question would be, "Well, what do I wear?"

"You girls know this website?" Sonia continued, pointing at her *Be Jane* shirt beneath the overalls.

"No," both girls responded.

"Well, I'll tell you what: Be-Jane-dot-com is all about empowering us girls to do the handiwork that we've always left to the guys. I painted the basement here last week, even the floor. This week I thought I was gonna have to spend hours stripping off the gross wallpaper in the kitchen, but then I read a Jane tip about painting right over it."

"That's what you're doing?" Alex asked nervously. "You're painting over the wallpaper?"

"I'm actually done," Sonia announced with a satisfied grin.

Alex led the way as we barged into the kitchen. Sure enough, our only known link to Aunt Arabella's world had been severed by the brush of a pretty painter. Sonia had done a thorough job, covering every square inch of the wall.

"What do you think?" she asked with pride. "That should make it a little easier to sell this place."

"It looks nice, but we actually liked the paper," I said. "It reminded us of one of those Magic Eye puzzles."

"Really?" she said with a shrug. "Well, I can never see those things anyway."

"So . . . we were just passing by on our way to the park and figured we'd see who was here," I said.

"Well, I'm glad I got to meet you," Sonia replied. "Thanks for keeping an eye on the old place. Oh, and let me warn you: There's a Looney Tunes lady named Evelyn Fields who lives next door. She'll probably be snooping around, but try to keep her away."

"What's wrong with her?" Aggie asked.

"Just weird and nosy," Sonia said matter-of-factly. "Oh, and she's got this raspy voice that just sets me on edge. I guess she used to be a pretty good singer back in the day, but she wound up having some vocal cord problems. Nodules or something. Thank God I'll never have to listen to her arguing with Aunt Arabella anymore. That's when her voice sounded the scariest."

"Did they argue a lot?" Alex asked.

"One minute they were great friends, and the next they were in a heated disagreement about politics or something. Personally, I think Evelyn was jealous of how much Aunt Arabella had achieved in life, especially since her own singing career had taken a nosedive."

"Mrs. Fields isn't dangerous, is she?" Mandy asked.

"Nah," Sonia said and swiped the air in front of her face. "Well, not unless you buy my theory about her husband. He was in the middle stages of Alzheimer's disease a few years ago, and Mrs. Fields was telling my aunt about how hard it was getting for her to take care of him. Next thing you know, he falls down their basement steps and dies. My theory is that she gave him a little push."

Mrs. Fields' metal cane flashed in my mind and I shivered. I also thought of poor Bobby Swenson, who had been pushed to his death so many years ago in North Dakota.

"Hey, let's trade cell numbers," Sonia continued and gingerly removed an iPhone 6 from her pocket, careful not to get any paint on the expensive device. "If anything happens here at the house and you're not able to get hold of my brother, then just call me."

Sonia and I saved each other's number in our phones. After that, we twins just stood there in the kitchen, staring at the wall as if our mental powers could coax Aunt Arabella's puzzle world to the surface of the paint. Finally, Sonia told us she had other things to do around the house, which we took as a polite signal to leave. On our way out, Alex asked, "Are you and your brother clearing out the place?" I knew what he was concerned about—that if they took all of Aunt Arabella's things away, we might miss out on a piece of important evidence.

"No," Sonia responded. "Actually, our real estate agent believes houses show better with a lived-in look. Plus, if it appears that someone still lives here, that helps keep away thieves. I've read about creeps coming into empty houses and tearing out the plumbing and even electrical wiring to sell as scrap."

Mrs. Fields was still sitting on her porch when we left, and we exchanged waves again.

"So now what?" Mandy asked as we walked down the street.

"We need time to think," Alex advised. "Let's go write down everything we know at this point and then plan our next step."

"My next step will be on the basketball court," I said.

"You can't still expect us to go to the park after what just happened at Aunt Arabella's!" Alex fumed. "I mean, seriously."

"Seriously, that's what I'm doing," I replied. The wall was painted and there was nothing we could do about that. Plus, we could discuss other strategies later in the day. Right then, my basketball team needed me. "Anyone care to join me?" I asked, looking at Aggie.

Alex's face went red with anger when Aggie raised her hand. I was happy that at least one of the other twins saw the situation my way. "It's no big deal," Aggie assured her brother. "We'll meet you back at the Cousineaus' when we're done."

Aggie and I peeled away from our siblings. I sneaked a peek at the time on my phone, hoping that we would arrive at the park before Sarah. I was also hoping that the two girls would get along okay.

"So, how dressed up does she get to watch a basketball game?" Aggie asked with a chuckle.

"Who?" I asked, pretending not to know who she meant. I had told Aggie about Sarah's fashion addiction.

"Miss Sarah Beasley," Aggie replied.

"Nothing special. Probably just what most girls would wear to prom." We both laughed and then I changed the subject. "Hey, now that I've got you alone, what's the deal with Dayton? Don't be mad at me for asking, but does it have something to do with your father?"

"I'm not mad. All I want to say for now is that it involves a special delivery to my father. Only he doesn't know anything about it yet. And neither does Alex. So don't say anything to your roommate."

"Oooh, very mysterious," I teased. True, Alex and I were roommates now, but at least we weren't sharing a bed like the girls were. My mom thought I was being such a considerate host when I insisted on sleeping on a cot in my room. Honestly, though, the thought of accidentally making contact with Alex during the night kind of freaked me out.

Aggie and I arrived at the fringe of Cain Park, and I was excited to show it off to her. It really is a cool place, set low in what my parents call an "urban valley" between two main roads: Lee and South Taylor. The park has a stage for live performances, tennis courts, skateboard ramps, and my beloved basketball court surrounded by fifteen-foot high fencing. Players were warming up on the court as Aggie and I descended the grassy hill. "Welcome to my world," I said with a sweep of my hand.

"Whoa! I have to admit this is a little different for me," Aggie said, sounding nervous. I looked at her through narrowed eyes, not sure what she was referring to. "I'm not used to being a minority," she whispered.

Now I looked at the scene from a white North Dakotan's point of view and saw exactly what she meant: Far more than half of the people in the park were African American. And it was pretty loud too, with kids already talking trash and laughing it up more than what you would find in a typical all-white crowd. Brandon, my best friend, is black, and he and I often joke about the differences between our cultures. "Y'all are just way too tight sometimes," Brandon says. "We wanna laugh, we laugh. We wanna sing, we sing. We're not looking over our shoulder to see if anyone approves."

Having grown up in an integrated neighborhood, I found the scene quite normal and welcoming. Aggie's comment didn't make me think any less of her, though, or assume she was racist. As my parents have taught me, people tend to fear unfamiliar people and unfamiliar situations. "Is it cool?" I asked quietly. "Should we stay?"

"Oh, of course," Aggie quickly responded with a forced smile. "I was just saying . . . Yeah, of course we should stay."

Sarah left a picnic table where she had been sitting with two girlfriends and walked toward us. She pointed at Mickey Mouse and called out, "You're on MC time once again." MC time—Mark Cousineau time—means I'm running late. At least she didn't look mad; she was probably more concerned about showing Aggie what a terrific girlfriend she was. Sarah kissed me and made a few clothing introductions. "Cora," she said, pointing to her white tank top; "Abigail," tapping her navy blue plaid shorts; "and Comfortable Junior," lifting a foot to show off her navy-striped flip-flops.

"And this is Aggie Burke," I announced. There stood Aggie in one of her standard summer outfits: untucked T-shirt, athletic shorts, and basketball shoes.

"Boy, you really *are* tall!" Sarah said and gave her a hug. "Come on. You'll sit with us."

As Sarah was about to lead a wide-eyed Aggie away, Brandon came sprinting over. "Man, am I glad to see you," he said, already sweating. "Now we're down only one player. Still no Rashad."

I introduced Brandon to Aggie. "Aggie could play for us," I offered and looked hopefully at her.

"Oh, that's okay," she said sheepishly. "I'll stay with Sarah." I knew that Aggie loved basketball and that she was used to playing against guys, so I figured she was either intimidated by the looks of the competition or she was just being polite to my girlfriend. Maybe it was a combination of the two.

"Of *course* she'll stay with me," Sarah proclaimed. "Sometimes you get the stupidest ideas, Mark. Aggie may be big, but she's still a girl."

That comment cinched Aggie's decision. "I'll play," she said with a wicked smile.

"What?" Sarah protested with her hands on her hips. Brandon and I laughed. "Well, go ahead then and get yourself killed," Sarah muttered. "What do *I* care?"

"Let me run down the house rules," I said to Aggie as we loosened up. "We play five guys a side—full court, not half. No subs. Once the game is started, what you got is what you got. Baskets inside the arc are good for one, outside the arc good for two. Call your own fouls, but only if it's really obvious. No foul shots, though; the fouled team just gets the ball. Play to fifteen and you gotta win by two. Got it?"

"Got it," Aggie responded seriously.

"Now, warn her about LeRon," I said to Brandon. I figured Aggie would take the warning more seriously coming from someone other than me. She might think I was just being overprotective.

"Everybody on the court today is going into eighth grade," Brandon began. "But you see that really tall dude with braids? That's LeRon, but he calls himself Le*Bron*. Anyway, he was held back a year in school—maybe even two. You're gonna want to stay clear of him as much as possible. He can be a real fool."

"Yo, DJ, let's get this pawty stawted!" LeRon called out and laughed his husky laugh.

"Give us a little time for shooting practice," I protested.

"You shoulda thought of that like twenty minutes ago," LeRon replied.

"See, I told you," Sarah called out. "Stupid MC time!"

How wonderful to have a girlfriend who disses me in front of LeRon Specter, I was thinking.

LeRon laughed and then stared at Aggie. "What? And now ya'll got a lemon meringue pie playing for you?" Aggie's shorts were yellow and her shirt was white.

"Shut up, LeRon," I said through gritted teeth.

"Make me, boy," he taunted. "And you can call me Le*Bron*."

"Start playing like him and maybe I will," I replied. "Even if you could play like his mamma I'd be impressed."

"Oh!" went up a chorus from my teammates.

"Big words from little Ten-Point-Eight!" LeRon laughed and chested up to me. I hadn't heard that rotten nickname in months. It was a mean reference to how fast I ran away one time when older boys were chasing Brandon and me. That had happened long ago, though—back in the sixth grade. I looked LeRon in the eyes and felt my muscles start twitching. I was nervous because I knew he could trounce me, but I wasn't about to back down. Fortunately, Brandon stepped in. "Let it ride, man," Brandon said and pushed us apart. And that's how the ritual plays out ninety-five percent of the time: Two guys go chest to chest and blow off some steam, and then another guy breaks them up. I've seen very few actual fights on the court. The real problems start when guys from a different neighborhood suddenly show up, and you know right away they're just looking to cause trouble.

The game got off to a rocky start for our team because Brandon, Tony, and Mike were doing all the work for us. Aggie wasn't moving with her usual, confident stride, and she looked nervous—like she was playing hot potato—every time she handled the ball. Seeing her so uncomfortable made me uncomfortable too, so I couldn't shoot worth a darn. LeRon and his boys were whooping it up, especially after LeRon slipped past our defense for a dunk. Our team was down five to one when Brandon tapped Aggie's shoulder and said, "Hey, don't hold back that North Dakota magic. Mark has been bragging on you for a year now!" And right there was an example of why Brandon is such a good friend and a good sport. Instead of getting upset with Aggie and me for not contributing points, he found a way to pump us up instead.

Aggie and I looked at each other and smiled. It felt like we were instantly transported back to University Park in Grand Forks, where the two of us had been unstoppable the previous summer. "Behind the arc," Aggie said with a confident nod.

We drove down the court. Tony passed to Brandon, who was far out on the baseline, and Brandon passed to me. I faked a drive to the hoop and dumped the ball off to Aggie, who was standing undefended behind the arc. *Swish!* "That's a two!" Mike called out.

"Lucky pie shot," LeRon mumbled.

We did the same thing two more times in a row because LeRon's team wasn't showing Aggie any respect, just leaving her to choose any old spot behind the arc. After the third swish, I called out, "Way to go, rainmaker!" and gave Aggie a big, sweaty hug. When I let go, I noticed Sarah's eyes boring holes through my body. *I guess I'm in trouble,* I thought for a moment, but then quickly got my head back in the game. With the score tied at seven apiece, Aggie suddenly had one of LeRon's boys stuck to her like glue. We all had to contribute, and I was happy to find that my shooting skills had returned.

The score was tied at thirteen now. Aggie was dribbling in place at the top of the key, guarded by LeRon and looking for an open man. LeRon's boys had us smothered no matter how much we moved. "That's right: no easy-bake shots," LeRon taunted Aggie. Then he made the fatal mistake of moving in too close to her. Aggie responded with a killer crossover that a young Dwyane Wade couldn't have executed any better: She did a head fake to the right, then dribbled between her legs to switch direction, driving to the left side of the hoop to rap in a lay-up. LeRon actually lost his balance and fell on his butt! Everyone laughed, including LeRon's own teammates. LeRon spent the next thirty seconds cussing us all out.

To make matters worse, LeRon then set off on a solo drive across the court, only to miss a dunkshot. The ball sprang high off the rim and into my hands. All we needed was a point to wrap up the win. I passed to Mike, and Mike dumped it off to Brandon, who missed a jumper from just inside the arc. Aggie came down with the rebound, and just as she was about to shoot, LeRon hacked her arm.

"Come *on,* man—foul!" I shouted. To be honest, I actually swore. I was upset to see Aggie wincing in pain and holding her left forearm. I touched her hand. "You okay?" I asked. She nodded.

"No blood, no foul," LeRon fumed, holding the ball. "If she gonna play *with* the dudes, she gotta play *like* the dudes."

"Foul," I said through gritted teeth. "Now give us the ball back."

"The rule is call *your own* foul," LeRon mocked me. "And so far, I ain't heard the little lady call *nothin'*."

"Call it," I said to Aggie.

"I don't want to win like that," she responded firmly. "We'll get it back on our own."

I knew there was no point in arguing with her, so we let LeRon's team keep the ball. Everyone on our team was fired up and determined to win for Aggie's sake; there was no way we would let them score again. And we didn't. Brandon pulled down the rebound like a pit bull going after a T-bone steak. For our final drive down the court, Brandon bounce-passed to Aggie, who threaded a one-hander to me between LeRon and another defender. I arced in the winning shot from twelve feet away.

"Awesome game!" Brandon proclaimed and threw an arm around my neck and Aggie's. We exchanged fist bumps with the players on the other team except for LeRon, who stormed off the court like a baby. I shook my head as I watched him leave. And that's when I noticed that the spectators' table was empty.

"Did anyone see when Sarah and her friends took off?" I asked, but no one did. Once again, I knew I was in trouble. I walked a distance away from Aggie and my other teammates to call Sarah on her cell phone.

"What?" Sarah answered, obviously annoyed.

"I just wondered where you disappeared to," I said innocently.

"What do *you* care? You looked like you were having a great time without me."

"Well, it was a good game. An awesome game."

"*Awesome*," she repeated sarcastically. "I'm so happy for you."

"Look, what's the problem?"

"I saw the way you looked at that girl and the way you hugged her."

"She was my teammate and she was playing great. So what?"

"And that's another thing. Why would any girl want to spend so much time playing basketball? Maybe she knows that's the only way she'll get close to guys. Anyway, I think the whole thing is just really stupid."

I stared at Aggie's profile while she took a long drink from the fountain. I couldn't deny that she meant more to me than Sarah did. Maybe not as a girlfriend, but as a person and a friend. No question about it. Still, I panicked at the thought of losing Sarah. I had gotten used to guys telling me how lucky I was to have her. I had gotten used to attractive girls eyeing me whenever I was out with her. Now, if a person has managed to win a gold-plated championship trophy, he shouldn't just toss it off the roof. Right? Wouldn't make sense.

This is what I felt like saying to Sarah: "You know what *I* think is really stupid? Clothes that have names."

And this is what I really said: "Look, I'm sorry I didn't pay more attention to you. I just got caught up in the game. I'll make it up to you."

"Okay, okay," Sarah sighed. I was relieved. "When does she leave, anyway?"

"Sunday."

"Well, don't plan on just abandoning me for the next five days. That wouldn't be fair."

"I won't. I promise."

"All right, then. Call me later. Promise."

I promised to call, and we said our good-byes while I walked over to Aggie.

"Everything okay?" Aggie asked.

"Fine," I responded with a forced smile. "Let's go home and get some ice on that."

I touched Aggie's arm and let my hand linger there. She smiled sweetly at me, and I instantly got an uneasy feeling in my stomach, like I was walking a tightrope.

CHAPTER SEVEN

Our twins were in the basement when we got home. Alex was pacing back and forth behind Mandy, who was seated at the keys of her laptop. They both had serious looks on their faces.

"Hey, you okay?" Alex asked his sister when he saw the ice pack.

"Fine," she said. "Just a bruise."

"We'll show you what we have so far," Mandy said. "See what you think." She printed a copy of the following table for each of us:

Assumptions:	1. Someone murdered Aunt Arabella.
	2. Coins and poison are somehow involved.

Suspects	Possible Motives	Details
Evelyn Fields	Jealousy	<ul><li>Argued with Arabella</li><li>May have mental health issues</li><li>Bitter about failed singing career</li><li>Looked violent when swinging cane</li><li>Pushed husband downstairs?</li><li>Easy access to Arabella's house</li></ul>
Sonia Jenkins	Inheritance money	<ul><li>Seems flighty</li><li>Easy access to Arabella's house</li></ul>
Jonas Hoffer	Inheritance money	<ul><li>First one to find Arabella after death</li><li>Easy access to Arabella's house</li></ul>

Aggie and I nodded our heads, impressed with how thorough our siblings had been. It was weird to see my science teacher's name as one of the suspects, but we couldn't rule him out.

"So where do we go from here?" I asked. "We can't go to the police and say, 'Based on two Magic Eye pictures we found on Arabella Hoffer's kitchen wall, we believe she was murdered.'"

"That does sound just a tad insane," Aggie laughed.

"We'll need to keep this all real quiet for now," Alex advised.

"Alex and I already Googled Aunt Arabella and the three suspects, but we didn't find anything that would help us," Mandy said. "We figure the best we can do is keep talking to the suspects as much as possible."

"Yeah, and hope that Aunt Arabella will be able to communicate with us in some way other than through the wallpaper," Alex added.

The whole situation was frustrating to me. If Aunt Arabella could lead two people to the same book, cause state birds to swoop down at two others, and project 3-D images through wallpaper, then surely she should be capable of other amazing feats. And then I remembered Bobby—he too had limitations to his powers, limitations that even he didn't understand.

"Who knows what Aunt Arabella's capable of?" Mandy asked as if reading my mind.

****

After supper, the four of us headed back to Redwood Road once again. The Escalade was no longer in the driveway, so that meant Sonia was out of our way. There was no sign of Mrs. Fields either. We marched in a quick single-file up to the door. I opened it with my key and then locked it behind us in case Mrs. Fields decided to pay a visit. The air inside was warm and thick with paint fumes. We went directly to the kitchen, where the smell was almost too much to take, but at least a fan was moving the air around. I gently tapped the wall and then looked at my fingers—no paint on them. We closed the shades to make it as dark as possible in the room. The stained glass window had no shade, but only soft, colored light filtered through it at that time of day.

We sat on the floor in a circle, making sure our knees touched as they had in the North Dakota launch control center when we summoned Bobby's energy. A whole year had passed since that séance, and now here we were again in the exact same boy-girl-boy-girl configuration. Mandy pulled a candle out of her backpack and lit it with a disposable lighter. Once she set it down in the middle, we all held hands.

"It's not very dark," Aggie whispered.

"It'll have to do," Alex replied. "Close your eyes, everybody."

We closed our eyes and just sat there in silence. The fan was one of those models that pivot from side to side, so every few seconds I felt a fresh burst of air on my back. The hum of the fan reminded me of the electrical hum in the launch control center, and once again I felt energy tingling through body. *Stay calm,* I told myself. *Don't let the others feel you shiver.*

"Aunt Arabella?" Mandy's whisper sliced through the silence and made my muscles clench. "We're here in your kitchen because we think you've called us together."

"We know you've communicated with us through the wallpaper, but now that's painted over," Alex said. "Give us some other sign that you're still available."

"Let's open our eyes in case we're supposed to see something," Aggie suggested.

Our hands were getting sweaty, but we continued to hold them anyway. We kept stock-still and waited for a response. Nothing. No, wait. Did the fan suddenly start spinning faster? Did water just drip from the faucet? Did I hear a squeak from the basement? And then came an unmistakable sign: The phone mounted on the kitchen wall started to ring.

"No way!" I yelled and broke free of the circle. I got to my feet. The phone poured out a continuous, lazy ring that couldn't quite hold a steady note. It was a quiet sound, more like a purr. "The phone line is *dead!*"

All of the twins were standing with me now, wide-eyed. "Are you sure?" Alex asked.

"I checked the first day I came in," I replied breathlessly.

"Answer it," Mandy directed, looking squarely at me.

"Why me?" I asked. The phone continued its drunken purring.

"You're in charge here," Mandy reminded me with a mischievous grin.

"All right, all right," I said and walked over to the phone. I put my hand on the receiver and felt a vibration trickle down to my elbow. I was woozy.

"Answer it!" Mandy repeated.

With one swift motion I yanked the receiver from its hook and thrust it to my ear. The ringing stopped and I winced in anticipation of what Aunt Arabella might have to say. I imagined her voice would sound gravelly, like Mrs. Fields'.

"Hello?" I said cautiously.

Nothing. Not even static on the line. The phone was as dead as the first time I had checked. "Hello?" I repeated more boldly. Same result. I held the receiver out toward the others and shrugged. One by one, each of them tried their luck at getting some kind of a response, but it was no use.

Aggie hung up the phone and we all looked at each other helplessly. We had reached a dead end, literally. If Aunt Arabella had the power to ring a phone from beyond the grave, why couldn't she send a message of some kind to tell us who killed her? The four of us stood in a loose huddle in the middle of the kitchen floor, just watching the fan turn its head from side to side. Mandy finally spoke. "Here's a thought," she began. "Aunt Arabella rang the phone to let us know she's still available, but maybe she's holding back other information from us on purpose. You know, just to see if we can solve the mystery with only a couple of clues."

"Excellent point!" Alex sang out and patted my sister on the back. "She was the consummate puzzler herself, and now she wants to see what we're capable of."

"Oh, great," I moaned. "So now we're rats in her maze and she's seeing how long it takes us to find the cheese?"

"Or the grain," my dear roommate corrected me. "Rats sometimes have a hard time digesting cheese."

"Whatever," I said. In any case, it was kind of creepy to think that Aunt Arabella was watching us. Even if she had been a terrific lady in her lifetime, I still wasn't thrilled about the current situation.

Suddenly, Aggie put a finger to her lips and held up her other hand. She had clearly heard something. The rest of us listened carefully, and there it was—someone unlocking the front door. I quickly opened the accordion door to the basement and waved everyone through. I closed the door quietly behind me and tiptoed down the stairs. With only a washer and dryer in the basement there was absolutely no place to hide, and with glass block windows there was no way to escape. If whoever just entered the house decided to walk downstairs, we would have been found out for sure. We put our backs to the wall that formed one side of the staircase and listened carefully. The visitor was heavy-footed up above, so we guessed it was a man. He walked into the kitchen and stayed still for a while. *Please don't come down the basement.* He clicked off the fan and then started climbing the stairs to the second floor.

"Let's go!" I whispered, and everyone followed me up the basement steps. We were as quick and quiet as panthers. I noticed a half-eaten bag of black licorice on the kitchen counter. "It's Mr. Hoffer," I announced to the other twins when we were clear of the house, and I explained how I knew.

"Perfect!" Mandy exclaimed. "Go back in and talk to him."

"I'm getting a little sick of being bossed around," I protested and stared at my sister. "Why does *bruh-boo* have to do everything?" I hoped that reminding her of the silly name she used to call me when we were toddlers would shame her into action.

"Pretend you're just stopping by to check on the house," Alex advised me.

"It *is* a good opportunity for you to nose around a little and see what Mr. Hoffer might have to say," Aggie said. I must have given her a *What, you too?* look. "Sorry," she added.

"Why can't we all go?" I asked.

"A bit suspicious," Alex concluded.

"Come on, Mark," Mandy pleaded. "You trust Mr. Hoffer, don't you?"

"Yeah, I suppose," I replied.

"Plus, we'll be waiting for you around the corner," Mandy assured me. "If anything goes wrong, just call my cell, okay?"

"Yeah, like if I need you to come remove a knife from bruh-boo's chest or something?" I whined.

"Stop being so dramatic," Mandy warned. "No one's going to stab you."

"Famous last words," I mumbled.

******

"Hello?" I called through the screen door. Mr. Hoffer was on the settee in the living room, holding a laptop computer.

"Mark? Hey, come on in," he said happily. "Checking up on the old house, eh? Boy, I do appreciate that."

He was making this easy for me.

"Have a seat," he said and pointed at one of the wingback chairs. As I sat down he held the bag of licorice out to me, but I politely waved him off. I wondered why the bowling trophy from the kitchen and the pocket knife from the den were now on the coffee table. *Great . . . so there is a knife involved.*

"My wife and I are heading to Virginia tomorrow to visit the in-laws," he explained and pointed a finger into his open mouth as though he wanted to puke. "My laptop tanked on me today, and I don't want to be without one for the trip. So, I figured I'd come over to get Aunt Arabella's."

"Oh," I said, searching for an opening to get more information. "That's pretty cool that a lady her age even had a laptop. Did she use it a lot?"

"Every day," he said proudly. "She wrote e-mails to friends and family, did puzzles, read articles, and even tracked her investments."

"I hope it's not too nosy to ask or anything, but did she have a lot of investments?"

"Old Aunt Arabella built up a pretty good nest egg for herself over the years, especially since she didn't have any children."

"I guess that part's good for you," I teased. "You're probably rich enough now that you don't have to deal with seventh-graders anymore."

"Rich?" he laughed. "Not really. Aunt Arabella left a fourth of her money to Saint Jude's Children's Hospital where they do cancer research. If there's one thing Aunt Arabella just couldn't stomach, it was the idea of a terminally ill child."

"Wow, that's really nice," I said. I felt a surge of pride for Aunt Arabella's generosity even though I had never met her.

"And as for the rest of the money," Mr. Hoffer continued, "my brilliant sister Sonia managed to lose two hundred thousand dollars' worth of it last year."

"What? How did she manage that?"

"Ever hear of a hedge fund?"

"No."

"Well, I don't know much about them either, other than that they're risky. Anyway, Aunt Arabella had always been a conservative investor. Her strategy was basically to follow the tortoise from that old fable. You know, the idea that 'slow and steady wins the race.'"

"Sounds smart to me," I said.

"To me too. But Sonia kept harping on her and harping on her about getting a better return on her investments. Finally, Aunt Arabella gave in and invested two hundred thousand in a hedge fund. And . . . long story short, she wound up losing the entire amount."

"Were you and your aunt mad at your sister?" I asked.

"Aunt Arabella was furious, and I must admit I was pretty upset for a while too. But then I figured, hating my sister isn't going to bring the money back. Plus, it was money that I never even earned. My wife and I are getting by okay on what we make now. So what the heck, you know?"

I nodded. I thought about Mandy and was grateful to have a smarter sister than Mr. Hoffer had.

"Anyway, now it's Sonia who's going to suffer the most from the lost money. Her ex-husband got her accustomed to a certain lifestyle: nice home, Cadillac, and yada-yada. That's why she wants to hold out until we get top dollar for this house. But enough of all this financial stuff; I must be boring you to tears!"

"No," I assured him. I pointed at the trophy and knife on the coffee table. "Are you taking those to Virginia as well?"

"No, I'm just afraid that Sonia will get it in her head to suddenly sell everything while I'm gone, and I want dibs on these."

"That's a pocket knife?" I asked innocently, as though I hadn't seen it before.

"Yeah. Have a look. The place she got it—Saint Michael's Lanes—closed before I was even born, but it had a special place in Aunt Arabella's heart for a couple of reasons. One, it's where she met the man who would become her fiancé. That's the most important reason. And two, she was the engineer who installed an automated pinsetter system there in the early 1950s."

"What do you mean by that?"

"I mean, Saint Michael's still had pin boys until then. Can you believe it? It used to be someone's job to wait on a little perch at the end of an alley and then set up the pins that were knocked down."

"What a crummy job!" I said and fantasized about Alex performing that role. There he was . . . a sweaty mess, pushing up his glasses and dodging flying pins.

"And what about the trophy?"

"Oh, that's the crazy part," Mr. Hoffer said with a laugh. "You're not going to believe this, but there's a very weird connection between the knife and the trophy. You know who Mr. Randall is—the pharmacist at the Lee Road CVS?"

"Oh, yeah," I said and pretended to puff on a cigarette. "I think everyone knows who *he* is."

"Well, Mr. Randall just happened to be a pin boy at St. Michael's at the time Aunt Arabella installed the automated system. Right up until my aunt died, Mr. Randall always teased her about taking away his old job. And as for the trophy, my aunt rolled her 178 in a championship game when her team was playing none other than Mr. Randall's team. Aunt Arabella's score put her team over the top!"

"How long ago was that?"

"Just a month before she died. I was there to watch. Boy, you should have seen Old Randall's face when Aunt Arabella rolled her final strike!"

"Did he say anything?"

"He just teased her again. He shook his fist at her and said, 'First you take away my job, and now you take away my championship!' Aunt Arabella got a real kick of that."

The wheels were spinning in my brain. Mandy and Alex had recently read a bowling-related murder mystery. Could this be another one in real life? "Do you think Mr. Randall was at all serious about being upset?"

"Nah. He comes across as really crabby to most people, but I think he actually has a good sense of humor. Aunt Arabella thought so, and she was a faithful customer of his for years."

Who has a better opportunity to poison you than your own pharmacist? I thought. "Oh, did she need lots of prescriptions?" I asked innocently, but my heart was pounding.

"No, just one for high blood pressure. She would never admit to having plain old high blood pressure, though; she always called it 'just a touch of the hypertension.' Other than that, she took an over-the-counter calcium supplement." Mr. Hoffer looked at his watch. "Hey, I need to get going. Thanks again for your help, by the way. The yard looks terrific."

"One question for you, Mr. Hoffer," I began. "I know you said your aunt had a lot of interests, and I was just wondering if coin collecting was one of them."

"Coins? Nope. Not to my knowledge. Why, are you a collector?"

"Sort of," I fibbed. "I'm just getting started, though, and wondered if she had any coin books I could borrow."

"Be my guest to look around, but I don't think you'll find any."

I followed Mr. Hoffer outside into the weak daylight. The other twins would be concerned about how long I was taking to get home. Mrs. Fields was out on her glider listening to a crackly old jazz recording. The singer was a woman with a rich, smooth voice that seemed to be sculpting the notes of the song.

"Good evening, Mrs. Fields," Mr. Hoffer called out.

She tossed us one of her salutes and flashed a smile that looked eerie in the faint light. Once again, I pictured her bashing in heads with her deceased husband's cane.

CHAPTER EIGHT

We officially entered Mr. Randall into our table of suspects and updated the Details column for Sonia and Mr. Hoffer:

Suspects	Possible Motives	Details
Mr. Randall	Revenge for losing old job Revenge for losing championship	- Could have poisoned medication - Seems antisocial and mean
Evelyn Fields	Jealousy	- Argued with Arabella - May have mental health issues - Bitter about failed singing career - Looked violent when swinging cane - Pushed husband downstairs? - Easy access to Arabella's house
Sonia Jenkins	Inheritance money	- Seems flighty - Talked Arabella into bad investment - Needs money for fancy lifestyle - Easy access to Arabella's house
Jonas Hoffer	Inheritance money	- First one to find Arabella after death - Easy access to Arabella's house - Seems to be very proud of Arabella - Not very concerned with money

We all agreed that Mr. Hoffer was the least likely suspect, so we would focus our attention on the others, especially since Mr. Hoffer was heading out of town. Also, we suddenly found ourselves in a time crunch. It was Wednesday morning already, and the trip to Dayton would take up the entire next day. With the Burkes flying back to North Dakota on Sunday, we knew we had to work fast.

Mandy had a batch of chocolate chip cookies in the oven before Dad even left for work. "You're torturing me with that smell," he complained while finishing his coffee. "I hope you remember to save a couple for me."

"Of course I will, Daddy," Mandy said sweetly. We were all together at the kitchen table except for Aggie, who was still in the shower. Mom and Dad thought it was wonderful of Mandy to bake cookies for Aunt Arabella's neighbor. "She'll be so surprised and happy for the company," Mom cooed. Naturally, Mandy didn't mention that the real objective for visiting Mrs. Fields would be to pump her for information about a murder case—one in which she herself was a suspect.

"Hey, since the lady's name is Mrs. Fields, shouldn't she be baking *us* cookies?" I asked with raised eyebrows. No one laughed. "Get it? Mrs. Fields? As in Mrs. Fields Cookies?"

"Very cute, honey," Mom said with zero enthusiasm. I swear, sometimes I don't know why I waste my A-material on these people.

"Will anyone have time to stop by CVS today?" Dad asked.

"Aggie and I are planning to go there," I said. "Why?"

"Good deal," Dad said and pulled out his wallet. He handed me eight dollars. "Would you get me a large can of athlete's foot spray? I'm all out."

"Aw, come on, Dad," I protested and tried to return the cash. "Can't you get that yourself?" I didn't say it, but I would be embarrassed to buy athlete's foot spray in the company of a girl. After all, we're talking about fungus that grows on smelly human flesh. Disgusting!

"So your father works all day, and then you expect him to stop at a store on his way home?" Mom chided me. "Don't be so inconsiderate, Mark, especially since you're going to CVS anyways."

"Yeah, what's the big deal, Mark?" Mandy asked. I absolutely hate it when she becomes an ally of our parents in order to gang up on me. I immediately shot a cold look at Alex of *Don't you dare join in too.* My poor roommate got so nervous that he choked on his milk. I put the money in my pocket and slapped Alex on the back a couple of times while he raised his hands in the air. "You okay now?" I asked ever so considerately. Maybe I hit him a little harder than was necessary, but it worked just fine.

The plan was to divide and conquer. Mandy and Alex would pay a visit to Mrs. Fields, while Aggie and I would do the same with Mr. Randall. Both girls would be armed with micro voice recorders in their canvas purses.

****

"Socks first," an old man's voice grumbled behind us, and the musty odor of smoke settled on us like cobwebs. It was Mr. Randall. I knew it before I even turned around. Aggie and I were standing in the CVS foot care aisle, and I held a different can of spray in each hand, trying to remember which brand my father preferred.

"Pardon me?" I said, avoiding eye contact.

"Make sure you put on your socks before your underpants," he advised. "That'll prevent the fungus from spreading from your feet to your crotch."

No way! There I was in a public place with a girl, and this old man had just made a reference to my crotch! I felt my face get hot as I searched for some sarcastic remark to shoot back at him, but nothing came to me. Mr. Randall flashed a yellow smile and chuckled as he walked toward the exit. He pulled a pack of cigarettes and a lighter from the pocket of his lab coat.

"It's for my father," I called out lamely.

Aggie put a hand over her mouth and pretended to cough, but I was sure I heard a muffled laugh. "What?" she asked innocently as I stared at her. She was having a hard time keeping the corners of her lips from twisting up into a smile.

"Let's pay for this and go have a chat with our old friend," I said, annoyed.

We found Mr. Randall in his usual position on the bench, smoking a cigarette. Aggie casually reached inside her purse to click on the recorder and then took the lead with our suspect. "Mind if we sit down, Sir?" she asked politely.

"Free country," Mr. Randall replied without looking at us.

Aggie plunked herself down closest to Mr. Randall and I sat on the other side of her. We endured a few moments of uncomfortable silence before Aggie elbowed me. "Mr. Randall, I'm Mark Cousineau—George and Brenda's son. We've been coming to this store forever."

"Okay, I believe you," he replied sarcastically.

Man, this guy wrote the book on being a smart-aleck! I was thinking. "And this is my friend Aggie from North Dakota," I continued. "Anyway, I'm taking care of the yard at Arabella Hoffer's place, and her nephew—her grandnephew, my science teacher—mentioned that you used to know her."

"Arabella Hoffer," he said with a smile and took a long drag on his cigarette. He made eye contact with me for the first time. "They don't make dames like that anymore."

"What do you mean, exactly?" Aggie asked.

"What I mean is that woman was a spark plug right up until the very end of her life—full of energy and interested in everything. The first time I laid eyes on her was in 1952. I was sixteen years old working as a pin boy in a bowling alley, and in walks this confident, attractive engineer lady. She was almost twice my age at the time, but boy did I ever have a crush on her!"

"You did? That's sweet," Aggie said.

"All of us pin boys did, even though we knew she was there to put us out of business. See, she was hired to install a pinsetter system in the place. I gave her guff about that whenever I saw her, right until the end. It was a running joke with us."

"You didn't really care about losing your job?" I asked.

"Only for a week," he answered with a shrug. "But then I found a job working at a little drugstore called Hagan's, right on this spot, and got to be pretty friendly with the pharmacist. He's the one who encouraged me to go to college, and the rest—as they say—is history." He pushed his cigarette butt in the hole of a long-necked receptacle and started hacking.

"You should really consider quitting," Aggie advised.

"Oh, boy. Now *you* sound like Arabella," he laughed. "She told me that every time she saw me.'" Mr. Randall shook his head and laughed again. "Now, if you'll excuse me." He stood up and started walking toward the store's entrance.

"One more thing," Aggie began boldly. "I'm a big fan of mysteries and I'm trying to write one myself, so I've been dying to ask a pharmacist this question: If one character wanted to poison another, what would be the best thing to use? You know, something that would do the job quickly and would be hard to trace."

This got Mr. Randall's attention. He stopped and looked at us with arched eyebrows. "Hm, very good question. I know exactly what *I* would use. That much is for sure." And then there was a maddeningly long silence.

"Well?" I prodded him.

"Oh, I'm not about to tell that to a couple of kids, and especially not to ones who mysteriously showed up at my bench. Who knows? Maybe you're planning to poison *me*, and I certainly don't want to be the one to give advice on how to do that. I may appreciate irony in my life, but not in my death." He flashed a grinchy smile and slinked into the store.

****

"And you decided to bake me cookies?" Mrs. Fields' voice asked suspiciously on Mandy's recorder while jazz played in the background. The four of us twins were at our dining room table listening to the recorded conversations of our suspects. My father was still at work and my mother was out somewhere, so we didn't need to worry about them overhearing.

"I bake a lot," Mandy fibbed on the recording. "I'm always sharing cookies and brownies with my neighbors, but today I thought of you instead."

"I see. Well, then, that's very kind of you," Mrs. Fields replied, sounding convinced. "Both of you have a seat here on the porch and I'll be right out with some fresh lemonade."

We sat through two minutes' worth of crackly jazz while Mrs. Fields got the drinks. I recognized the singer's voice as the one I had heard the previous night when leaving Aunt Arabella's house.

"There you are," Mrs. Fields finally said. "Now, let's have a taste. Mm-mm! Very good cookie. Wonderful. And believe you me—with a name like Mrs. Fields, I know a thing or two about cookies."

Both Mandy and Alex laughed on the recording. I threw my hands up in the air, thinking, *Oh sure, it's suddenly funny when she says it.*

"That's nice music," Mandy said.

"Guess who's singing? That's me from many, many years ago. That's a demo record I made at a studio right here in Cleveland."

"Wow, you really had a great voice," Alex said.

"I thank you," Mrs. Fields replied. "'Course, it never amounted to a hill of beans once I started having throat troubles. I mean, before that I had my share of singing in local clubs with some pretty terrific musicians, but that's about it."

"Sonia Jenkins from next door mentioned that you were a singer," Mandy observed, setting the bait.

"Sonia Jenkins?" Mrs. Fields repeated with disgust in her voice. "What in the world are you talking to her for?"

"We stopped by the house with my brother, and she was there painting," Mandy explained.

"She's a snooty one, I don't mind telling you," Mrs. Fields said. "Nose always up in the air like she thinks she's better than everyone else. Even Arabella said the same thing about her."

"Really?" Alex asked. "The two of them didn't get along?"

"They weren't together all that often, but when they were, they tended to argue a fair amount. See, Arabella wanted Sonia to become less concerned with material things in life and more concerned with developing her mind. Arabella herself was an accomplished engineer with wide-ranging interests, and she wanted to impart some of that zest for knowledge to her grandniece."

"So, that's the kind of thing they argued about?" Mandy asked.

"Yes, and believe you me, there was no joy in it for Arabella. The kind of argument she liked to engage in was all about ideas. Lord knows, she and I got into many a spirited one ourselves! But, like sisters, we quickly made up afterwards. And that's what Arabella was to me—like a big sister. I really looked up to that woman." Mrs. Fields' voice quavered even more than usual.

"Aw, you must really miss her," Mandy said.

"I do. I've got pretty much no one now. My husband's gone. All my other relations live out of town. So . . . Well, anyway, that's my lot in life. If Arabella were here right now, she'd say, 'Evelyn, you make your own lot in life. It won't do you or anyone else any good to wallow in self-pity.'" And then Mrs. Fields actually laughed.

After a pause, Alex asked, "When was the last time you heard Aunt Arabella and Sonia arguing?"

"You kids call her Aunt Arabella? That's sweet! She'd get a kick out of knowing she's acquired bonus nieces and nephews. Anyway, the last argument . . . That would be about a week before Christmas. I was tossing something in the trash bin when Sonia's big old Cadillac turned into Arabella's driveway. Arabella got out of the vehicle, and I heard her say, 'Fool me once, shame on you. Fool me twice, shame on *me*. I refuse to be drawn into another one of your shady deals, and that's final.' Arabella slammed the door and marched into her house. Sonia pulled out of the driveway like a bat out of . . . Well, let's just say she left in a hurry."

"Did you get to ask Aunt Arabella what all the commotion was about?" Mandy asked.

"I did the very next day. But she just accused me of being nosy, as she often did. I brought it up again on

Christmas Eve, but I got the same response and we just went ahead with our gift exchange. She gave me one of those iPod music gadgets. Still in the packaging. Maybe one day you can show me how to use it?"

"Oh, sure," Mandy said.

"No problem," Alex added.

"And I gave her the same thing as always: a membership renewal to the Cleveland Museum of Art and a fresh Christmas caramel pie," Mrs. Fields said. "Simple pie, really, with pecans and loads of caramelized sugar. But that Arabella absolutely adored my Christmas caramel pie!"

The recording went on for several more minutes with conversations that had nothing to do with our case. For example, Mrs. Fields had Mandy and Alex talk about their favorite subjects in school. She also shared pictures of her children and grandchildren. Finally, she described the fun she and her husband had every summer when they rented a house on the Outer Banks of North Carolina.

****

After listening to both recordings, we decided that neither Mr. Randall nor Mrs. Fields was our prime suspect. Both of them seemed to have a lot of respect for Aunt Arabella. Mr. Randall claimed to know which poison he would use to kill someone, but we believed he said that to mess with us. He was creepy and obnoxious, but that didn't necessarily make him capable of murder. As for Mrs. Fields, she was lonely without Aunt Arabella. Would it really make sense for her to remove her "big sister" from this world? No.

"Two things, though," Alex began. "One, the reason for murder doesn't always have to make sense. And two, maybe two or more of our suspects joined together to do the deed."

"That's possible," Mandy agreed. "Maybe Mr. Randall was the source for the poison, but one of the others fed it to her."

We decided that Sonia was our prime suspect since she had the strongest motive for committing the crime: greed. We needed to find out exactly what the "shady deal" was that Aunt Arabella had referred to only a week before her death. We had a hunch that it had something to do with coins.

CHAPTER NINE

Aggie and I sat in the back seat of the PT Cruiser while my father drove us down to Dayton. We had reached the outskirts of Columbus—more than halfway to the Air Force Museum—when Dad cranked up his *London Calling* CD by The Clash and started singing along. Overall, my father is a pretty cautious person who works hard to provide for his family and his students. He's the kind of guy who goes to church every Sunday, pays bills on time, and obeys every law. However, he still has a rock & roll streak that jolts to the surface occasionally. "When they kick at your front door, how you gonna come?" Dad belted out. "With your hands on your head or on the trigger of your gun?" He was pretty much spitting the words. Aggie started laughing, and I just rolled my eyes.

I decided to take advantage of our privacy in the back seat. I leaned in close to Aggie's ear and asked, "So why are we really going to Dayton?" She reached into her purse and pulled out a silk pouch with a drawstring at the top. She opened it and took out a rectangular medal with a black border, a gold background, and a white Chevy logo—like a bowtie or a stretched out addition sign—in the middle.

"It's a hood ornament from an old Chevy truck," she explained.

"Okay. And?"

"Let's just call it a Father's Day gift a few days early," she said mysteriously and returned the medal to its pouch. So I had been right that the hidden purpose of our trip was to see her father. I was surprised, though, that she would bring him a present. The man had abandoned her, her twin brother, and her mother, so why give him anything? I was afraid that Aggie had a fairytale scene in her mind, expecting her broken family to suddenly reunite and live happily ever after. But she obviously didn't want to say anything more about her plan, so I backed off.

We must have gone through a cell phone dead zone somewhere between Columbus and Dayton because I suddenly received a voicemail from my girlfriend. She was ticked. "Well, this is really stupid," Sarah's message began. After a pause, the rest of her words tumbled out: "Here it is, almost noon on Thursday, and I'm wondering where you are. I told myself I wouldn't be the one to call since I seem to remember something about a promise *you* made to call *me*. Oh yeah, and that was two days ago, by the way. But, I couldn't help myself. So, here I am calling you like an idiot. Where are you? Are you having an *awesome* time with your *awesome* little friend from North Dakota? Or, I guess I should say your *big* friend from North Dakota. Anyway, I'm not sure if this whole . . . thing is working for me. It's all really stupid. You said you were gonna call, right? When were you planning to get around to that? I swear, Mark, sometimes I'm not convinced you realize what you have. And if that sounds conceited, tough! It's the truth. So . . . here's the deal: I'm expecting a call from you before five o'clock today. If you don't call by then, then don't call at all."

Aggie was listening to her iPod, so at least I didn't have to say anything to her about the message. Sarah had started a time bomb ticking in my head, and it was set to go off at

5:00 PM. *Who does she think she is?* I sneered. I was so close to calling her on the spot and just blasting her. But then I wimped out. Parts of what she said were true. For one thing, I did promise to call her; I just never said when that would be. Two days didn't seem like a big deal to me, but I guess it was for her. For another thing, Sarah was right that I was lucky to have a girl like her. *Still, you can't let her talk to you like that,* a part of me said. *She's walking all over you, dude!*

I could hardly enjoy our tour of the Air Force museum because I kept wondering what I would eventually say to Sarah. Aggie was as quiet as I was, and I figured she was thinking about the Chevy medal in her purse and searching for the right moment to put her plan into action. My father, though, was like a hyper kid in a candy store. For over two hours he happily led us from one giant gallery to the next, sharing details on everything from a Wright Military Flyer (1909) to a Boeing B1B Lancer (1988). "Now we're really talkin'!" he proclaimed as we entered the Missile & Space gallery, where the ceiling was over a hundred feet high to allow room for towering missiles. A simulated launch control center was also on display, and while it wasn't exactly the same as the one I had visited in North Dakota, it was very close. Sitting in the commander's seat made me think of Bobby Swenson and brought back the excitement of solving the mystery of his murder with the other twins.

Aggie's mind was in the same place. She smiled at me and said, "It's hard to believe it's been a whole year already." And then she turned to my father. "Mr. C, thanks again for taking us here."

"You're more than welcome, honey," Dad replied. "In case you hadn't noticed, I've been enjoying myself too."

"Now, here's the thing," Aggie said and bit her lower lip. "I haven't been completely honest with you about why I wanted to come here today. I mean, the exhibits are great and everything, but . . . well, I was hoping I could see my father."

"Your father?" Dad asked in shock and actually looked around the gallery. "He's here?"

"I did a little digging and found out that he's with the 88th Mission Support Group here at the base," Aggie explained.

"I see," Dad said seriously and nodded his head. He knew as much about Aggie's father as I did: that he had met another woman ten years earlier while away for training; that he divorced Aggie and Alex's mother; and that he had been completely out of their lives ever since.

Aggie pulled an index card out of her purse. "See, here's his number," she said and handed the card to my father. I saw what she had written and was confused by the name, Tech Sergeant Ryan Anderson. "His last name's not Burke?" I asked.

"Burke is my mother's maiden name," she said. "She took her own name back and gave it to Alex and me after our father was gone for a couple of years."

Dad put his hand on Aggie's shoulder. "Sweetheart, what is it you hope to get out of this?"

"I want to see him one more time. It's just . . . I feel like I have to do this. Just see him for a minute, give him something, and then we can be on the road. It won't take long, I promise."

"I'm not worried about the time," Dad assured her. "I'm worried about *you*. I don't want to see your feelings get hurt. It's been so long since you were a part of his life. This will be a huge shock for him."

"It doesn't matter," Aggie said with a determined look on her face. "This is something I want to do for *me*, not for him."

I looked at the two of them and felt a rush of pride. I was proud of my father for trying to protect Aggie, and proud of Aggie for being so committed to her plan. Dad finally gave in with a sigh. "Okay, so what do you need me to do?" he asked.

Aggie was ready with a response: "Call that number, identify yourself as Captain Cousineau, and say you have a package for him from Grand Forks, North Dakota."

"Okay, so I guess you *have* given this some thought," Dad chuckled. "But how do we get to him? Anyone can get into the museum, but the rest of the base is secured."

"You still have an Air Force Reserve card, don't you?" Aggie asked. She knew that my father was still in something called the Individual Ready Reserves.

"Yes, but I'm not sure that would get me access to an operational unit here," Dad explained.

"Maybe you could ask him to meet you somewhere," I chimed in. "Like here or at the main gate."

"That's a good idea," Aggie agreed.

"Sounds a little suspicious to me, but I'll give it a try if you really want me to," Dad offered.

"Please," Aggie said and forced a smile.

We decided the call would be more convincing if it came from a base phone instead of a cell phone, so my father ducked into a museum office while Aggie and I waited out in the hallway. Aggie refused to sit on a bench with me even though we had been on our feet for hours. She stood there with her arms folded and jiggled her knee up and down.

"You okay?" I asked.

"Nervous," she replied. "But this is something I need to do."

Aggie's words inspired me. "You know what? There's something I need to do too," I announced and stood up.

"I'll be right back." I walked into the Missile & Space gallery and took out my phone. I had bars. No wimping out now.

"Well?" Sarah answered.

"Well, I beat your five o'clock deadline," I said sarcastically. "You should be thrilled."

"What do you have to say to me?"

"Same thing you said. Two times in your message you used the expression 'really stupid.' So I just wanted to share with you what *I* think is really stupid: clothes that have names and girls who care more about their outfits than they do about other people."

"What?" Sarah fumed. "Who do you think—"

"Here's what I think you should do," I interrupted. My heart was racing. In my mind I was climbing to the top of the 108-foot Titan II missile with sweaty hands, barely maintaining a grip on my championship trophy. "You should introduce a pair of white socks to a pair of pink sneakers and then take a hike in them." The trophy crashed to the ground.

"Oh, that's real mature," Sarah sneered.

"I guess I'll see you around," I said, and I didn't mean it sarcastically. I wasn't holding a grudge against Sarah. She definitely had her good qualities, but I was suddenly happy and relieved to be out from under her thumb.

"Whatever," she said and hung up.

I jammed the phone in my pocket and walked back confidently to Aggie.

"Anything important?" she asked.

"Nah," I replied. "Everything's cool."

When my father walked out of the museum office and saw us, he pursed his lips and slightly shook his head. He reminded me of a surgeon arriving in the waiting room to console family members.

"What?" Aggie asked with wide eyes.

"He's away right now, and they're not sure if he'll be coming back to the unit today."

"Did they say where he is?" Aggie asked.

"Well . . . Aggie, you're not going to like this. I guess his wife called from the BX parking lot and said she was having car trouble. That's where he is—he went over to help her."

Aggie's face was frozen. "So, I guess he married her," she said as though in a trance.

"Let's just head home," I suggested. I felt sorry for Aggie and angry at her father for messing up her reunion plans.

"Great idea," Dad agreed. "We'll stop at any restaurant you guys want along the way. Aggie's choice."

"Hold on, Mr. C," Aggie said. "Will your ID card get us to the BX?"

"Well, yes," Dad reluctantly admitted. "But are you sure that's the best idea?"

"It's the *only* idea," she declared and led the way toward the museum exit.

****

The late afternoon sun was beating down on the asphalt parking lot of the base exchange—the BX—which is a department store for military families. We saw a man in uniform cranking a jack to lower a cherry red Chevy Impala to the ground while a woman and two young boys, around six and eight years old, looked on. My father pulled into a spot one aisle away, facing the Impala. The man was at least 6' 2" and had a perfectly bald head.

"That's him," Aggie announced in a half-whisper. My heart fluttered, and I couldn't imagine what Aggie's heart was doing. Not only was she seeing her father again for the first time in ten years, but she was also seeing half-brothers that she hadn't known existed. My world would be turned upside down if my parents suddenly announced they had more kids than just Mandy and me.

"Another flippin' nail," Sergeant Anderson raged. He actually used a curse word in place of *flippin'*. "You're unbelievable, you know that?"

"Oh, like I run over nails on purpose," the woman shouted back. She was wearing tight denim shorts and a halter top that matched the color of her car. She had bleach-blonde long hair and appeared to be younger than the sergeant. Both boys had disgusting mullet haircuts: short in the front, on top, and on the sides, but down to their shoulder blades in the back. They were chewing up sunflower seeds and spitting the shells on the ground.

"Just stay out of the flippin' construction areas," Sgt. Anderson shot back and used the back of his hand to wipe sweat from his forehead.

"Excuse me for trying to find us a decent new house," the woman said sarcastically.

Sgt. Anderson put the jack in the trunk and slammed it shut. "As always, it's been a real pleasure," he said with equal sarcasm while wiping his hands on a rag.

The woman hustled her two boys into the car and peeled out of her parking spot. Sgt. Anderson tossed the rag in the back of a black Chevy pickup truck with an *Ain't Skeered* bumper sticker. He walked to the driver's door.

"Lets' go, let's go!" Aggie urged.

The three of us got out of the PT and took a few steps toward the truck. "Excuse me. Sergeant Anderson?" my father said cautiously.

"Yeah, what?" he grumbled.

My father extended his hand and walked closer. "I'm Captain Cousineau, and I have someone here who wants to talk to you."

"Oh. Sorry, sir," Sgt. Anderson said, straightening up. He checked to make sure he was grease-free before shaking my father's hand. I guessed he didn't salute because my father wasn't in uniform. "I didn't mean to be rude. I just finished up a little family situation. I'm sure you know how that goes."

"Hm," Dad grunted, refusing to agree with him.

"Anyway, someone wants to talk to me?" Sgt. Anderson asked suspiciously.

Aggie stepped forward, and I knew from the fire in her eyes that she wasn't looking for a fairytale reunion. "I see you're still a Chevy man," she said bitterly.

Sgt. Anderson snorted. "Okay, so do I know you?" he asked.

"Not at all," Aggie said and took another menacing step toward the sergeant. "You haven't seen me in ten years. You haven't done anything for me in ten years. Or for my brother. Or for my mother."

Sgt. Anderson squinted and put his hand on the side of the truck as if to keep himself from falling over. "My God," he whispered. "Aggie, is it you?"

"Oh, so at least you remember my name," she responded coldly. "Yeah, it's me. And I'm not really sure why I'm standing here right now, other than to tell you that we've done fine without you."

"Aggie!" he said desperately and tried to put a hand on her shoulder. She pushed it away.

"Actually, I'm pretty sure we've done *better* without you," she continued in a raised voice. "Alex is the smartest kid in North Dakota and I'll wind up getting a basketball scholarship to college. Our mother just finished her degree and has a great job. And she's still really pretty."

"I can explain," Sgt. Anderson pleaded. "I never wanted to be cut off from you kids. It was your mother; she wouldn't even accept my child support checks after a while."

"Don't you *dare* blame any of this on my mother," Aggie exploded while jabbing the air with an accusing finger. "You never even tried to come back to see us. Not even once. My only connection to you has been this." She pulled the silk pouch from her purse and slid out the Chevy hood ornament.

"I always wondered what happened to that," Sgt. Anderson said and gazed reverently at the medal. "That's all I managed to save after some idiot totaled the truck that went with it. First truck I ever owned."

"I found it years ago," Aggie explained. "My mother told me to throw it away, but for some reason I hid it. You know why I brought it here today? I planned to throw it at you. No lie—throw it right in your face. But I won't do it. You know why? Because my mother raised me better than that."

"I appreciate that, believe me," Sgt. Anderson said with a forced smile. "You look like you could throw pretty hard." Then he held his hand out. "Any chance I could have that back? It kind of means a lot to me."

His words infuriated Aggie. "It means a lot to you?" she yelled. "Well, maybe if you knew where it's been all these years, you would have found the time to come and visit it. You want it back now? That's great. Go get it."

Aggie cocked her arm and then whipped it forward. The medal gleamed as it shot through the air, clearing the front of the BX and landing somewhere on the roof. Sgt. Anderson was still staring in that direction when Aggie threw the silk pouch at him. It puffed against his chest and landed at his feet.

"I'm ready to go now, Mr. C," Aggie announced and led us toward the PT Cruiser.

"Hey, wait!" Sgt. Anderson called out, following us. "Aggie, don't just leave like this. I'm your father, and you came all this way to see me."

"You had a chance to be my father," Aggie corrected him. "Not anymore."

Sgt. Anderson put a hand on each of her shoulders. "Aggie, come on."

"Don't you touch me," she hissed and wriggled out of his grip.

"Aggie, come on," he repeated desperately. Once again he put his hands on her shoulders.

My father pushed his hands away this time. "Look, the young lady made it clear she doesn't want you touching her," Dad said forcefully. "Get in the car, kids."

We did as we were told and climbed into the back seat. My knees were shaking. I was afraid my father would wind up getting seriously hurt by this sergeant, who was younger and bigger than him. And then if my father went down, would the man try to pull Aggie from our car and take her with him? You hear about crazy stuff like that where broken families are concerned.

"Who *are* you anyways?" Sgt. Anderson asked, glaring at my father and blocking his access to the driver's door.

Dad didn't flinch, and the determined look in his eyes said he wouldn't back down for anything. "Me? You want to know who I am? I'm just a guy who adores that girl in the car, and there's nothing I wouldn't do to protect her. That's all you need to know." And then he added through clenched teeth, "Move. Now."

The tense standoff continued for several seconds, but Sgt. Anderson finally stepped to the side. My father got in the PT without saying a word, and we drove off. I was so relieved that he didn't get hurt, but then I feared the incident wasn't really over because the sergeant followed us outside the main gate. I knew my father was aware of his presence because he kept checking the rear-view mirror. Dad's glare was intense, and I could see little spasms in his jaw as he clenched and unclenched his teeth. Finally, after at least three miles, the sergeant's truck turned down a side street.

We were all completely silent in the car; not even the radio was on. I put a hand on Aggie's knee as a sign of support, but she just continued looking straight ahead in a daze. I was so sad for this girl and so impressed with the strength she had displayed.

"Stop the car!" Aggie suddenly called out. "I'm gonna be sick!"

My father swerved into a roadside park and pulled into a spot in front of a two-sided outhouse. We all got out of the car and Aggie dashed into the women's side of the building covering her mouth. I was really concerned now.

"Should I follow her?" I asked.

"Let's just give her some time to herself," Dad advised.

We sat on a bench in the shade. I was aware that a girls' softball team was practicing and that little kids were laughing on a nearby playground, but all I could focus on was the door that Aggie had entered. I just wanted her to come back out and be fine again. But when she did finally reappear, she looked pale and weak. My father and I jumped to our feet and hurried over to her.

"Let's sit for a while," Dad said, and we led Aggie to our bench. Dad and I sat on the two ends, leaving room for Aggie in the middle. She continued standing. "Honey, have a seat," Dad said, but she still didn't. Then he gently pulled her onto his lap and held her close. Aggie snapped out of her trance and began to cry, just sniffling at first, and then letting it all go. "It's okay, sweetheart," Dad said and stroked her hair. "Shh."

I moved in close to them and felt tears run down my cheeks.

CHAPTER TEN

Only three of us twins were at the breakfast table the next morning because Mandy was already babysitting the wonderful Linden kids. Alex raved about his visit to the Einstein show, speaking enthusiastically about exhibits on light, time, gravity, and energy. His favorite was an interactive blackboard that demonstrated how mass can be converted to energy and energy to mass—in other words, $E = mc^2$.

"You two didn't have much to say when you got home last night," Alex said. "Was it a good trip to Dayton or not?"

"It was worthwhile," Aggie said matter-of-factly. Aggie had decided that she would keep her meeting with their father a secret for now. She planned to tell Alex and their mother about it when they were all together in North Dakota.

"That's all I get is *worthwhile* after I shared all those details about Einstein?" Alex asked. He was appalled.

"I was thinking ahead, Alex," I said. "On my dresser you'll find a map of the museum and spec sheets on some of the most famous aircraft."

"Cool!" Alex responded. "I can keep them?"

"They're all yours, roommie," I assured him. "But for now, don't we have work to do? I mean, you guys are leaving in two days."

"I know," Alex said. "For starters, I'd like to go with you to Aunt Arabella's. I want to check something out. Let me get my shoes."

"How you feeling?" I asked Aggie when Alex had disappeared. I thought her eyes still looked a little puffy.

"Better. You know what? Give me directions to where Mandy's babysitting. Maybe spending some time with little kids will help me clear my mind."

"Just don't *lose* your mind," I warned. "Those boys are wacky every day, so I can only imagine what they'll be like on a Friday the thirteenth."

****

I have to hand it to Alex: He was actually very helpful to me at Aunt Arabella's, doing all the weeding and edging while I mowed the lawn. Mrs. Fields must not have been home because her place was all closed up and she wasn't out on the porch. When we finished our work, I led the way into the house and went right to the kitchen.

"Maybe there's something cold to drink," I said and opened the refrigerator. The only item in there was a pitcher of water. I held it up in triumph. "Better than nothing," I declared.

"I wouldn't drink from that," Alex said. "Seriously, you don't know what might be in it."

"From six months ago? Come on, Einstein. Wouldn't the water have evaporated by this time, even in the fridge?"

"The pitcher has a lid, so you'd have a virtual water cycle within it. A nice, slow cycle because of how cold it is in there. Some water vapor would have escaped the container, but not much."

"But if this water is poisoned, wouldn't someone else have drunk it by now? I mean, Mr. Hoffer and Sonia have been in and out of here."

"If you're that eager to drink some, go ahead. When you suddenly fall into apoplexy, I'll be sure to call 911 for you."

"Apo- *what?*" I asked. Sometimes Alex's vocabulary is too much to take. I didn't know exactly what *apoplexy* meant, but from the context I knew it couldn't be very good. I stared at the clear, cold water. Part of me wanted to show up Boy Genius and just chug it down, but a bigger part of me was afraid. Before I could change my mind, I quickly removed the lid and dumped the entire contents of the pitcher in the sink.

"Okay, you may have just literally poured evidence down the drain," Alex said, shaking his head. "Who knows if some crime lab would eventually want to test that for poison?"

"Oh, too bad," I said. "That sounds farfetched to me anyway."

I got myself a glass of tap water. Alex did the same and then led the way upstairs, where he went right for the medicine cabinet. Mr. Hoffer had been right about Aunt Arabella's having only one prescription. Alex opened the bottle of hypertension medication and emptied the contents into his hand: two white capsules with a purple ring around each one.

"Very good," Alex said and gently shook the capsules like dice. "I was hoping we'd find capsules instead of solid pills so we can open them up."

We also found in the medicine cabinet a daily pill organizer, labeled Sunday through Saturday. The little compartments for Sunday and Monday were empty—flaps open—but the remaining compartments were closed. "That makes sense," I observed, "because I remember this past Christmas was on a Tuesday. Aunt Arabella would have taken her final dose on Monday, Christmas Eve." I carefully popped open the five flaps to find a capsule in each, identical to the ones Alex was holding, along with solid calcium tablets.

"Excellent," Alex declared. "We'll open all the capsules at the desk and see if any of them have a different looking powder in them." Alex's theory was that if someone did poison Aunt Arabella by using her medication, he/she may have only doctored up a couple of the capsules and left the rest of them normal. He thought this might be true for two reasons: 1.) The poisoner may have been able to obtain only a small amount of the deadly substance; and 2.) The poisoner may have wanted Aunt Arabella to unknowingly play a kind of Russian roulette with her pills.

"See if you can find little plastic bags down in the kitchen," Alex said. "Preferably Ziplocs. We want to keep each specimen separate."

I didn't appreciate being bossed around in the house I had been hired to protect, but I did as Alex asked anyway. He annoyed me, but I had to admit that he was always thinking of the details. For example, if I had been in charge of opening the capsules, I would have dumped all of their contents into a single heap.

I found an open box of sandwich-sized Ziplocs in a kitchen drawer and brought them to Alex in the den. He sat at the desk like a concert pianist waiting for the conductor's cue to begin playing. A lamp was shining brightly on his workspace where he had neatly arranged seven green note cards, blank sides up. He had also managed to find a magnifying glass and a metal nail file.

Alex gently twisted open the first capsule and poured its white powder onto a card. He leaned over the specimen to inspect it with the magnifying glass while using the tip of the nail file to move it around. "Nothing unusual here," he announced. I took a turn looking through the glass as well. It was just grainy white powder.

"How do we know what we're looking for?" I asked.

"We don't know exactly," Alex admitted. "We're just looking for any differences between the capsules."

"I remember my dad talking about some really powerful white poison that comes from a bean plant," I said, trying to impress Alex.

"That would be ricin," Alex replied casually. "It's distilled from castor beans."

"You think that's maybe what we're dealing with?"

"It better not be. If you breathe in just a few grains of that stuff, your life could be over."

I stared at the small mound of powder and made a conscious decision to begin taking shallower breaths.

Alex continued, "The good news is that it's pretty hard to make ricin and handle it properly. Plus, if Aunt Arabella had been poisoned with it, I don't think Mr. Hoffer would have said he found her all peaceful in her bed."

"Why not?"

"Ricin causes seizures, bloody vomiting, and severe diarrhea."

Alex's words painted a ghastly, smelly scene in my mind, and I shuddered at the thought of anyone leaving this world in that condition. "Say no more," I said. "So maybe it was some more common poison, like arsenic."

"Maybe," Alex allowed. "But even arsenic has pretty painful effects that might show on the face of the deceased. Same thing with strychnine."

Alex continued the capsule work until all seven of them were open, each on a separate note card. We were unable to detect any differences among the specimens, which led us to three plausible conclusions:

- All seven of the capsules were filled with nothing but medication; or

- All seven of the capsules were filled with the same poison; or
- One or more of the capsules contained poison, but detecting it would require an instrument more sophisticated than a magnifying glass.

We decided to bag up our specimens and take them home for safekeeping, just in case we ever needed to turn them over to the police. As I pulled the first Ziploc from the box, we heard someone calling from downstairs. "Hello?" the woman's voice said. It certainly wasn't Mrs. Fields' scratchy voice, and it didn't sound like Sonia's either. "Anyone in there?" I had left the main door open when we entered the house, so I figured the woman was calling through the screen door.

"Not again!" I whispered to Alex. We had a habit of getting caught in that house at awkward moments. I had a right—and even a duty—to be there, but now it looked as though we had converted the den into a meth lab. A regular drug den.

"Stall!" Alex whispered.

"I'll be right there," I called out and went bounding down the stairs. A plump woman in her thirties was standing on the front stoop with a young couple behind her. "Hi, can I help you?" I asked through the screen door.

"I'm Sue, the real estate agent," she announced with a genuine smile. She held up a business card for me to see.

"I'm Mark, the . . . the landscaper," I said and held up the keys dangling from the lanyard around my neck. I was happy to have a job title and keys; they put me on an equal footing with Sue.

"Well, you're doing a very nice job with the yard," Sue said. "I didn't want to come barging in and scare anybody, but I *would* like to give these nice people a tour of the place now. Okay?"

"Oh, sure," I said and held open the door.

I exchanged nods with the couple as they followed Sue inside. "Now, I know your main concern is the size of the bedrooms," Sue said to her clients, "so we'll start up there and if you like what you see, we'll work our way back d—"

"Hold on!" I quickly interrupted. "You're better off starting in the basement and working your way up."

"Oh, really?" Sue said, pursing her lips. "And why is that?"

"Okay, because . . ." I began. *Think, think.* I lowered my voice to a whisper and pointed upstairs. "This is really embarrassing, but my friend was helping me with the landscaping work today, and right now he's up there using the bathroom." Then I raised my eyebrows and fanned a hand in front of my nose.

"Just wonderful," Sue said and glared at me. I imagined the young couple making a mental note to replace the toilet seat.

"I'm really sorry," I told Sue. "We had no idea anyone was coming today. I'll make sure he sprays."

"Okay, folks, let's make this a bottom-to-top tour," Sue said with a forced smile.

Once Sue and her troops disappeared down the basement stairs, I scurried up to the den. I needed to work fast because showing that empty basement would take only a minute. Upstairs, Alex had finished bagging all seven specimens and was pushing them into the pockets of his cargo shorts.

"Do I need to hide?" he whispered and pointed at the walk-in closet.

"No, it's just a realtor showing the place," I said.

"And they know I'm here?"

"Yeah, it's cool. I told them a friend helped me with the yard work today." And then I lied to good old Alex: "I said you were up here fixing a lamp that had shorted out."

"Got it," Alex said and gave me the thumbs-up. He really had repaired an old lamp at my house earlier in the week. My dad was carrying it down to the tree lawn for trash collection, but Alex rescued it. My mother was delighted because the lamp had been in her family for years.

We walked out of the den and Alex headed straight for the stairs, but I made a quick detour to the bathroom. I flushed the toilet and sprayed Lysol in the air. Alex was waiting for me on the second step down.

"What did you do *that* for?" he asked.

"Oh, Mr. Hoffer asked me to flush every time I'm here. Just to make sure the plumbing is working properly."

"Makes sense."

"And, as you can see, the kitchen is freshly painted too," Sue was telling the couple when we got downstairs.

"Hi, I'm Alex," my North Dakotan friend said and extended his hand. No one wanted to shake it. The young man finally made a fist and bumped it against Alex's.

"Well, is it safe to go upstairs now?" Sue asked coldly.

"Safe?" Alex repeated. "Oh, yeah. The lamp works fine now. No chance of it shorting out."

"What?" Sue asked, obviously confused.

I made serious eye contact with Sue and tapped the temple of my forehead, making sure Alex didn't notice. Sue nodded knowingly. "That's nice that the lamp is okay now," she said sweetly and patted Alex on the shoulder. "Thank you for telling us, honey."

"Oh. Uh, sure," Alex said, looking more confused than I had ever seen him. His glasses were a little cockeyed on the bridge of his nose, and I imagined Aunt Arabella observing the whole scene and getting a good laugh out of it. I was having a hard time not laughing myself.

"Well, we should be going," I said. "I hope you like the house. It's a really nice place."

"So long," Alex said. I put a hand on his back and led him outside. "Jeez, what was the matter with those people?" he asked when we were clear of Aunt Arabella's yard.

"Who knows? Some people are just weird."

CHAPTER ELEVEN

It was Friday night and the four of us twins were brainstorming ideas in my bedroom. Thunderstorms had rolled through the area earlier, but now rain just pattered pleasantly on the roof. The girls sat on my bed, I sat on the cot, and Alex paced back and forth. He was agitated. We all were, really, and for a good reason: The Burkes would be leaving for North Dakota in less than forty-eight hours.

"I wonder if the poisoner used something that took advantage of Aunt Arabella's high blood pressure," Alex offered. "One of our uncles has high blood pressure, and he told me he looks for warnings on medications all the time: 'Check with your doctor before using this drug if you have high blood pressure.' Like that. It's all about avoiding a heart attack or a stroke."

"Good point," Aggie agreed. "Poison doesn't have to be something that would kill a rat. Even if someone used a legal drug on Aunt Arabella, it was still poison to her system."

"Hold on a second," Alex said and lunged over to the desk. He pulled my laptop to the edge so he could use it while still standing, and then checked the WebMD site for medications that people with hypertension should avoid. The list was surprisingly long: everything from over-the-counter pain relievers, decongestants, and herbal supplements, and on to a whole slew of prescription drugs.

As it turned out, one of the herbal supplements that can interfere with blood pressure medication is licorice! Naturally, we all thought of Mr. Hoffer. But the image of him feeding rope after rope of black licorice to his great aunt seemed farfetched and even a little comical. *Just twenty more of these babies, Aunt Arabella. That's it, sweetie—chew and swallow, chew and swallow.*

"Plus, that's just all sugar and artificial flavors," Mandy said. "I'll bet there's no real licorice in that candy anyway."

"Let's check," Alex said and Googled Twizzlers. "Hm, did you know Hershey's owns Twizzlers? Anyway, it says here that the strawberry, chocolate, and cherry-flavored Twizzlers do *not* contain licorice extract. But the black licorice ones *do* contain both licorice extract and anise oil."

"Still," I began, "there's just no way Aunt Arabella was Twizzled to death. Come on!"

"It's highly unlikely," Alex allowed. "But we'll still keep this in the back of our minds."

"So where do we go from here?" Aggie asked. "We still have nothing solid."

"We should go back to the house now and see if Aunt Arabella will give us any more information," Mandy suggested.

"We could do that," I agreed. "Or, what if we just flat-out challenge our suspects? You know, tell them we have evidence Aunt Arabella was poisoned and that the motive had something to do with coins. And then see how each one reacts."

"That would sound pretty crazy from their perspective," Alex said, but not like he was dissing me. "Plus, wouldn't they ask to see the evidence? I know *I* would if I were in their position."

"We could fake a note written by Aunt Arabella that we can say we found under her bed," Aggie offered.

"Yeah, I guess we could find a sample of her writing somewhere in the house," Mandy said.

"Or it could even be printed out from her laptop," I suggested.

"I don't like the whole note idea," Alex concluded. "Written or printed out, it just doesn't make much sense. I mean, if she thought she had been poisoned and still had enough energy to write a note, why wouldn't she call 911 instead?"

We had to agree with Alex on that point. We decided to follow Mandy's suggestion—to see what else Aunt Arabella was willing and able to share with us. The trick would be getting out of our house. It was already ten o'clock and my parents wouldn't want us roaming around in the dark. I decided to take advantage of Dad's OCD streak.

My parents were watching *Friday the 13th* in the family room when I started the time bomb ticking. They were dressed in pajamas, snuggled together on the couch. "Guys, sorry to interrupt," I said. "But I know I opened a window at Ms. Hoffer's today, and now I don't remember closing it. I should really get back there. The others will come with me."

"What?" Dad fumed and clicked the Pause button. Jason, the psychotic killer of Camp Crystal Lake, was staring at us through the eyeholes in his hockey mask. "How could you do something like that, Mark? I mean . . . come on!"

"I'm not sure I did," I replied innocently. "But I might have. Sorry."

"I'm sure you closed it, honey," Mom assured me. "Just check in the morning. Plus, from what you've told me about the next-door neighbor, she'll keep an eye on the place."

I could see Dad's breathing become heavier as he stared at the screen and did his best to ignore the situation. "Dad?" I said and looked at him with raised eyebrows. "What do *you* think I should do?"

"Listen to your mother," he barked and restarted the movie.

"Okay," I said sweetly and returned to my bedroom. "Poor guy," I said to the other twins. "I give him about ten minutes."

Mandy laughed. We could both picture him stewing in the family room, completely unable to enjoy the movie. Sure enough, we heard the knock on my door in eight minutes.

"Come on," Dad said with a sour look on his face. "I'll get dressed and run you over there now."

"No way!" I protested. "You're in the middle of a movie. Just relax, Dad. It's only two streets away and I'll have three other people with me."

"It's raining," he reminded us.

"Not like before," I replied. "Plus, we have umbrellas."

"Well . . . are you sure?" he asked hopefully. This would be a win-win situation for him and he knew it: 1.) Relief in knowing that Aunt Arabella's house was secure, and 2.) Relief in not ticking off Mom by abandoning her on the couch.

"Positive, Daddy," Mandy chimed in. "We'll take care of it."

Dad left my room a happy man.

****

Aggie and I shared an umbrella while Mandy and Alex did the same. I try not to be superstitious, but when Friday the thirteenths come around I find myself being extra cautious throughout the day. Now there I was walking at night, in the rain, to a haunted house on Friday the thirteenth. At least the moon wasn't full. It was half, and it only peeked out from behind the dark clouds from time to time.

"Good thing I have a candle in my purse," Mandy said when we reached Redwood Road. "Looks like we'll need it for more than just a séance." All of the houses were in the dark, with the exception of flickering candlelight here and there. There was no sign of life in Mrs. Fields' home and we assumed she would be sleeping by now.

"Lightning must have blown a transformer," Alex said.

We had planned to enter the house in the dark anyway to avoid alerting Mrs. Fields, and now Mother Nature had made our job easier. We crept through the front door like cat burglars. I quietly locked up and we stood in the entryway for a while to let our eyes adjust to the dark. We made our way into the kitchen where we set our umbrellas in the sink and sat down in our familiar circle on the floor. No one said a word. Mandy struck a match that sizzled to life, projecting an eerie, dancing glow on her face. With the candle now lit we remained in silence, listening to the soothing trickle of rainwater through the downspout just outside the kitchen door. Nothing and no one in the room seemed completely real, bathed in that dreamy candlelight. I was somehow scared and relaxed at the same time. My head felt a little buzzy.

"Aunt Arabella?" Mandy said quietly. Aggie and I gasped, squeezing each other's hand. I closed my eyes. "We're back again," Mandy continued.

"And we're running out of time, Aunt Arabella," Alex said. "Aggie and I need to go back to North Dakota day after tomorrow, and we really want to help you before we do."

"We got your first two clues about coins and poison," I heard myself say. "Can you give us some other information?"

"Or at least some guidance on what we should do next?" Aggie added.

No response within the house; just silence. Outside, though, thunder suddenly rolled and grumbled in the distance.

"Could that be for us?" I asked and opened my eyes. Everyone opened their eyes.

"I don't know," Alex replied with a shrug.

We waited expectantly for a few long minutes, straining our ears and eyes to pick up any sign Aunt Arabella decided to offer. Nothing. Inside the house there was only silence, and outside the rain had stopped completely. The clouds must have scattered because more moonlight began filtering through the windows.

"Maybe tomorrow we'll have better luck," I offered. It was getting late and I knew my father would be calling us any minute now.

"Let's at least have a look around the place before we leave," Alex said. "Maybe she's left a clue for us in one of the other rooms."

I slid open the accordion door to the basement and led the way down carrying the candle. The flickering light reflected off the freshly painted floor as if it was ice. We found nothing out of the ordinary downstairs, even after checking inside the washer and dryer. We went up to the second floor and snooped around in the bathroom, bedroom, and den. Again, nothing.

"Hold it!" Alex suddenly blurted out, startling all of us.

"Don't *do* that!" Aggie said and slapped him on the chest.

"Maybe Aunt Arabella is waiting for a sign from *us*," he announced with a wry smile.

"What?" I asked.

"You know," Alex continued, "some proof that we've been working on the mystery and that we're not just waiting for her to give us all the answers."

"That makes sense," Mandy agreed. "She wouldn't get any satisfaction from laying out all the puzzle pieces for us and then putting them together by herself."

"So what do we do?" Aggie asked.

"Do you have a copy of our table of suspects with you?" Alex asked his sister.

"Yeah, right here in my purse," she replied.

"Maybe that's all we need," he said excitedly and went bounding down the stairs in the faint light. We all followed. My cell phone vibrated when I was in the middle of the staircase, and I had to grab the handrail to keep myself from tumbling. It was a text:

`Why so long? Everything ok?`

"It's Dad," I told Mandy. "I'll stall." I texted him back:

`Mopping up water in the basement. Coming home asap.`

We didn't take our usual seats in the kitchen. Instead, Alex set the candle on the countertop closest to the recently painted wall and used the light to read from the printout. Alex looked like a lawyer who was practicing for a big trial by pleading his case to the kitchen wall. He discussed each suspect in detail, explaining what had aroused our suspicion about each one in the first place, and then sharing how we weighed the evidence.

"In conclusion," Alex finally said, "we have determined that our prime suspect is Sonia Jenkins, your grandniece. She had the motive of greed to keep up her fancy lifestyle. She had talked you into one bad investment and was trying to talk you into yet another one, most likely dealing with rare coins. She had a history of arguing with you. And, finally, she had easy access to you and to your house."

The wall was silent. After a minute, Alex threw his hands up in surrender. He had done all he could do. "Well, I guess we should go," he said with disappointment.

I squeezed Aunt Arabella's lanyard—the same one she had worn for so many years—and got up the courage to address her again. After all, as her official landscaper and house-watcher, I had a more direct connection to her than anyone else in the room. "Aunt Arabella, we've been working hard on this case for you," I said sincerely to the wall. "You yourself might not even know for sure who caused your . . . passing, but do you agree with our conclusion—with what Alex just said? In other words, who do *you* think did it?"

A blinding light suddenly whooshed in through the stained glass window and struck the center of the wall. *Where did that come from?!* It couldn't have been lightning because the skies had cleared and we heard no thunder. The light—still balled up in the center of the wall—began thumping like a heartbeat. And then it seeped outward in all directions until the entire wall pulsed with a glow-stick green fluorescence! The four of us backed away as far as possible.

"Whoa!" I gasped. "How's it doing that?"

"Maybe . . . the Compton Effect!" Alex announced with wonder in his voice. And then he continued breathlessly: "You remember that picture of Aunt Arabella with the Comptons from Wooster? Well, I've done some research on the Compton Effect. It has to do with high energy— gamma-rays and x-rays. When they hit other matter, like the wall here, they release electrons from the surface of that matter. Released electrons are causing this glow!"

"Wow!" was all that the rest of us could say.

And then the paint on the wall started to blister. It gurgled and oozed like lava until a puddle of the stuff formed on the floor, still glowing. The smell of fresh paint filled the air, and Aunt Arabella's original wallpaper was exposed once again. We got as close to the wall as we could without stepping in the ooze, which provided enough light for us to attempt a Magic Eye reading.

"There we go, Aunt Arabella," I said. "Now, who do you think did it?" *Relax and let your mind take it in,* I told myself. *You've done it before.*

"What the heck is *that* supposed to mean?" Mandy complained. She had obviously seen the 3-D image first. I shushed her. "Hm," I heard the Burke twins say. I shushed them too. Finally, after literally sweating for about thirty seconds, here's what I saw from left to right: a bullhorn, a plus sign, and a thumbs-up.

"Bullhorn and thumbs-up?" I asked, and they all nodded their heads.

"It's a rebus!" Alex declared.

We wracked our brains trying to solve it. *Bullthumb. No, Bullup.* If we had a suspect with the last name "Billups," for example, we would have been all set. But we didn't, so we had to keep trying. *Hornokay. Bullright. Horngood. Speak up.* Nothing was making sense. And then I did my best to "think outside the box," as Dad likes to say. I asked myself what the first object is used for, and the answer was to amplify sound. *Sound.* Also, what do people usually say when they give a thumbs-up? Cool! or Awesome! or Yes! or Yeah! *Wait a minute . . . yeah!*

"Sound Yeah!" I blurted out. "Get it? Like *Sonia*! Sonia killed Aunt Arabella!"

"That's it!" Aggie said and slapped my back.

"What do we do now?" Mandy asked.

"It's time to get Mr. Hoffer and your parents involved," Alex suggested.

"Mr. Hoffer's still in Virginia," I reminded him. My phone vibrated again. "Oh, and speaking of parents...." I fished the phone out of my pocket and was shocked to discover that the text wasn't from Dad after all. "No way!" I gasped. "It's from *her*. It's from Sonia." I read the text aloud:

Right behind you.

"That's creepy," Aggie said. "What's that supposed to mean?"

And then we heard tapping on the kitchen door. We turned around to find Sonia staring at us through the glass, her face bathed in the glow of a battery-powered lantern! We all screamed. Before we could move, Sonia unlocked the door and threw it open. She stood still for a moment, as though modeling her red rain slicker. Then she jolted across the room.

"What have you done?" she hissed and held her lantern close to the wall. The puddle of paint wasn't glowing anymore and wasn't in a liquid state either. It had cooled into rubbery lumps. Sonia kicked at the lumps with the pointy toe of her leather boot, but they were stuck to the floor tiles.

"We didn't do anything," I said innocently. "We stopped in to see if I accidentally left a window open here, and all of a sudden the paint started dripping from the wall."

"It must have been a weird chemical reaction," Alex offered.

"You know what's weird?" Sonia asked mockingly. "How about this? I'm driving by my great-aunt's house to make sure no one is robbing the place, and I notice a light in the kitchen. You know what's even weirder? Finding trespassers inside who claim that I killed her. That, to me, is very weird indeed." Obviously, she had been standing outside the door for longer than we had thought.

"It's just a silly game we were playing," Mandy claimed with a forced laugh. "I read a lot of mysteries and I'm a big fan of the old show *Murder, She Wrote*—you ever watch it?—and I guess I kind of pulled the rest of these guys into a game."

"Nice try, but I don't buy it," Sonia replied with a smirk. "Tell me what you know and how you know it."

"It was just a game," I repeated boldly, "and we apologize if you got the wrong impression. About the wall . . . I have no idea what happened, but if you and your brother want to fire me over it, fine." I began to remove the lanyard from my neck when my phone rang. "There's my dad," I announced. "We need to go."

"No, you need to *stay*," Sonia snarled and snatched the phone before I could answer. Now I was really ticked. "What the heck, lady?" I said and held my hand out to her. By now Dad had been sent to voicemail, which would freak him out.

Sonia slid my phone in the left pocket of her slicker and pulled a little gun from the right! We all gasped. My muscles shivered and I felt like I couldn't breathe. I flashed back to the previous summer when we had found ourselves in the same basic situation. I prayed that we would be as fortunate this time around.

"Please don't hurt anybody," I heard myself say in a shaky voice. "Just let us go and we won't say anything about this to anyone."

"Oh, that really makes me feel a whole lot better," Sonia said with a sarcastic laugh. And then she nodded at her gun, which was only the size of a 3" x 5" index card. "Isn't this adorable?" she asked. "It's an LM4 Semmerling by American Derringer. Teeny, but it packs a forty-five caliber punch and holds five rounds. Plenty to go around." Then she pointed the gun at us in a sweep. "Okay, let's have the rest of the cell phones."

Aggie and Mandy reluctantly handed theirs over. Sonia made Alex turn his pockets inside out to prove he wasn't hiding one. "I share the one phone with my sister," Alex truthfully stated.

"How very sad," Sonia replied.

Mandy's phone started ringing and Sonia looked at the face of it. "Daddy!" she said with a chuckle. "That's sweet."

"He knows where we are and he's gonna come looking for us," Mandy warned.

"Good point," Sonia agreed. "I guess I'll have to warehouse you somewhere else until we get this all sorted out."

I hated the sound of that word *warehouse*. I pictured a meatpacking warehouse where sides of beef hang from large hooks, and I didn't want us hanging there with them. I made quick eye contact with each of the other twins, one by one, and felt courage start to seep back into my system. Together, we were strong.

"You carry the lantern, Mr. No-Cell," Sonia ordered Alex.

"I have a real name," he replied indignantly. "It's Alex."

"Okay then, Alex," Sonia said sweetly. "Be a sport and carry the lantern for us. Let's move, everyone." The phone on the kitchen wall started its unbroken, drunken ringing. "What?" Sonia exclaimed. "There's no service here!"

"It's Aunt Arabella," Aggie announced while staring at our captor.

"Don't be an idiot," Sonia snapped. She put her hand on the receiver and left it there for a few moments, as if trying to find the nerve to answer. Finally, she yanked the receiver to her ear. "Hello? Hel-*lo*?" She looked smugly at Aggie. "See? The line is dead."

"Yeah, and so is Aunt Arabella, thanks to you," Aggie shot back.

We suddenly heard a rushing sound from the living room, as though someone had turned on a shower.

"Now what?" Sonia asked with a disgusted look on her face. She used her gun to wave us into the living room. A blue glow seeped through the doors of the TV cabinet, even though electrical power was still out. "Open it," Sonia demanded.

As soon as I swung open the doors, the screen changed from snowy static to a close-up of Aunt Arabella blowing out candles on a cake. I recognized this as the final scene from the *Our Lady Is 80!* DVD. Instead of fading out, though, the scene continued. Aunt Arabella looked directly at the camera—directly at Sonia standing there in the living room—and said, "You can't just throw a person's life away. Even though I was over ninety years old, my life still had value. At least *I* thought it did. Shame on you, Sonia." And then Aunt Arabella just stared straight ahead, silent.

"How are you doing this?" Sonia raged. "Turn it off!"

I pressed the power button first on the TV and then on the DVD player, but nothing happened. Aunt Arabella's eyes were still fixed on Sonia, seeming capable of burning holes right through her body. "Remove the disc!" Sonia shouted. I ejected the DVD, but with the same results. Sonia lunged toward the TV and slammed the doors shut. "We're outta here!" she said. "This house is a loony bin. Always was." Sonia was frazzled now. Her eyes were wide open and her hand shook as she shooed us back into the kitchen.

"Don't do anything else stupid, Sonia," Aunt Arabella called out from the living room. "I promise, you'll regret it if you do."

"Move!" Sonia yelled at us. "I know you kids rigged up this whole thing. I'm not stupid." She gave Alex a shove toward the door. He carried the lantern and led the way out to the patio.

We were greeted outside by a gravelly cry: "Yah!" A long metal object flashed toward us from the side of the house. It was Mrs. Fields! She struck Sonia's left shoulder with the cane, but not with enough force to make her drop the gun from her right hand. Sonia winced in pain and pointed the derringer at Mrs. Fields. The old lady held the cane high over her head, ready to deliver another blow.

"Hit me again and you're dead!" Sonia warned through gritted teeth. Mrs. Fields lowered the cane. Sonia grabbed it and whipped it out onto the back lawn.

"I'm sorry, kids," Mrs. Fields said breathlessly. "I saw there was something going on here, but I never dreamed it would be anything like this. Sonia must be insane!"

"Oh, that voice!" Sonia said with a shudder. "We'll have to take care of that right away. You know what, old lady? You just saved us all a ride in my Caddy. We're coming over to your place instead."

Sonia stayed behind everyone, directing us to the front of the house and across the lawn to Mrs. Fields'. I noticed that the Escalade wasn't in the driveway; Sonia had parked it in the street several houses away, most likely so she could sneak up on Aunt Arabella's place after noticing the glow.

As soon as we entered Mrs. Fields' front door, Sonia ordered her to find a roll of duct tape. "Don't you dare hurt these kids," Mrs. Fields warned her. Then Sonia forced Alex and me to tape her mouth and tape her arms and legs to a dining room chair. "We are *so* sorry," we said. Mrs. Fields looked more worried for us than for herself.

Sonia directed us twins to the basement, which had wood paneled walls and Astroturf carpeting. It was damp and musty down there; the air was thick. Sonia made us sit on an afghan-covered couch that faced an ancient TV with a rabbit-ears antenna on top.

"What are you doing?" Sonia asked when she saw Aggie reach into her purse.

"Can I get a cough drop?" Aggie asked innocently.

"*May* I," Sonia corrected. "Go ahead." Aggie did take out a drop, but I knew she must have clicked on her recorder as well. Sonia removed her slicker and dropped it to the floor. She was wearing jeans and a grey, ribbed T-shirt. She parked a wooden chair two feet in front of the couch, spindles closest to us, and sat on it backwards. She was facing us like a hotshot interrogator in a movie. As much as I tried to ignore it, I couldn't help noticing how nice and fresh she smelled. She rested her arms on top of the chair, aiming the derringer lazily to the side. With the eerie lighting of the lantern, it felt like we were on some kind of bizarre campout with a mentally twisted scout leader.

"Once again, tell me what you kids know and how you know it," she began. "And no stupid lies, please. You wouldn't yell 'Sonia killed Aunt Arabella' as part of a game."

The other twins looked to me as the official spokesman for the group. I decided to just go for it—to lay out what we knew and maybe get Sonia to fill in some gaps for us along the way. I didn't see a better alternative. After all, she was the one holding the gun.

"We know about the bad investment you got Aunt Arabella into," I began. "The one where she lost two hundred thousand dollars. Your brother explained that to me."

"Way to go, Jonas," she said with a roll of her eyes.

"We also know that you were trying to get Aunt Arabella to invest in coins," I continued.

"Foolproof investment," Sonia declared. "If she had bought a hundred and fifty thousand dollars' worth of those coins and agreed to hold on to them for just one year, she would have earned a twenty percent return. Minimum. The dealer I was working with practically guaranteed it. But how'd you know about the coins? I never told anyone about that."

"We saw them in the wallpaper that you painted over," Mandy said. "It was a Magic Eye image that Aunt Arabella sent us."

Sonia cracked up laughing. "The wallpaper," she scoffed. "Yeah, right!"

"Believe what you want to believe," Mandy responded testily. "You asked for the truth and we're giving it to you."

"That's how we found out about the poison too," Aggie added.

"Poison?" Sonia repeated. "Well, then, that's where your wallpaper lied. There was never any poison involved."

"Maybe not poison, like arsenic or strychnine," Alex began. "But you gave Aunt Arabella something she shouldn't have taken with her high blood pressure."

"Really?" Sonia mocked. "I would never harm a hair on dear Aunt Arabella's head."

"We know you were after her money," Alex persisted. "So you gave her some kind of stimulant to cause a heart attack or a stroke."

"Did not," Sonia replied like a second-grader on the playground.

I decided to use a little reverse psychology on her. "You know what, guys? I believe Sonia," I said. Then I looked directly at her. "No offense, but you don't seem like the kind of person who could plan something like that and pull it off without getting caught."

That comment set her off. She jumped to her feet and shoved the chair to the floor. "Adults underestimate my intelligence all the time because of the way I look," she snarled, glaring at me. "No way I'm gonna take it from a kid!"

"I apologize," I offered. "I just didn't think . . . Well, you know."

"Yeah? Well, think again, buddy," Sonia shot back and began pacing in front of us. "How about this for a plan? For the whole week before her death, Aunt Arabella was taking nothing but sugar pills."

"What?" I asked.

"I personally opened each capsule in her pill box and replaced the medicine with powdered sugar," Sonia explained. "I set it up the same way for the last two days of her life. And I thought ahead, too. I didn't touch the capsules for the remaining days or the ones still in the prescription bottle, just in case the coroner decided to investigate her death. That's what you call acting with prudence."

"So her high blood pressure *did* wind up killing her," Alex said.

"Yeah, but with a little nudge," Sonia said. She seemed to be very pleased with herself. "At night on Christmas Eve, I parked my Escalade way down the street and came to the kitchen door so nosy old Mrs. Fields wouldn't see me. I first apologized to Aunt Arabella for arguing with her. Then, while she was making tea, I cut us each a piece of caramel pie and spiked her whipped cream with three tablets of pseudoephedrine that I had crushed up at home."

"Pseudoephedrine," Alex repeated. "That's in medicine for colds and flu."

"Ding, ding, ding," Sonia said with a laugh. "We have a winner, folks!"

"My uncle can't take it because of his high blood pressure," Alex continued.

"And there you have it," Sonia concluded. She set the chair back up and sat as she had before. "Aunt Arabella went to bed with a full tummy and with warm feelings about our relationship. She had a good, long life and died in her sleep. For goodness' sake, that's all any of us can ask for, isn't it? She never suspected anything."

"That's where you're wrong," Mandy said firmly. "If she never suspected anything, she wouldn't have contacted us."

"Contacted you?" Sonia asked with a snort. "What kind of a crazy thing is *that* to say?"

"She did," Mandy insisted. "She found a way to bring us all together to work on this case. You wouldn't understand."

"I wouldn't, and I don't," Sonia replied. "Well, now I guess I can kiss my share of the house money goodbye when this place finally sells. But at least I have enough to get out of the country and make a fresh start."

"Where will you go?" I asked, thinking ahead to when the FBI would be searching for her.

"None of your business," she snickered. "I'll tell you where *you're* headed, though. There's an abandoned building just off Chester where I'm gonna park you guys while I make my exit. I'm sure someone will find you within a couple-few days. Oh, and I suppose we'll have to bring old Mrs. Fields along as well. If you're nice, I'll promise to keep the tape over her mouth."

I heard a knock at the door upstairs. I know Sonia did too because she froze and put a finger to her lips. "Not a word," she whispered.

"Is anyone home?" my father called out. Mandy and I looked hopefully at each other. Dad must have checked for us at Aunt Arabella's and then decided to come next door when his search was unsuccessful. Poor Mrs. Fields whimpered and moaned in response. Sonia *tsk*ed and pointed the gun at each of us to emphasize that we needed to keep our mouths shut. She was fidgety in her chair.

"Are you okay in there?" Dad called out with concern. "I think I hear someone." Then, after a pause and another whimper, he announced, "I'm coming in."

We heard him try to open the front door, but it was locked. "Here's how we're doing this," Sonia whispered hurriedly. "When he comes around to the back, I say *go* and we climb upstairs quickly and quietly. We leave by the front door and run to the Escalade. Got it? We leave the old lady behind."

It was difficult to see through the glass block windows because of the diamond pattern etched into them. I could just make out enough to know that Dad was heading to the back door. He shined a flashlight through one of the windows, but it was as though the light had to travel through several layers of cobwebs before reaching the basement. There was no way Dad could have seen us. He then knocked on the glass. "Anyone down there?" he called out desperately. I felt a little rattle in my throat—the beginning of an automatic response to my father—but I swallowed hard instead. I didn't want anyone to get hurt. Dad abandoned the window and continued moving.

"Okay," Sonia whispered, standing up. We stood up as well. "Ready, set—" Before she could say *go*, she was interrupted by a loud crackle. Electricity began arcing between the two metal ears of the TV antenna, starting at the narrow base and sizzling up to the widely separated tips. A science exhibit had suddenly come to life in Mrs. Fields' basement. And then Aunt Arabella's face zapped into view in the middle of the TV screen! Only she was the young Arabella/Madonna this time, appearing as beautiful and full of life as she did in the old photograph with her soldier fiancé. Aunt Arabella didn't say anything now. She just glared at Sonia.

"Aunt Ar. . . How?" Sonia babbled. That's when she made a critical mistake: She took her eyes completely off of us and aimed her derringer at the face on the TV. Aggie sprang into action, absolutely leveling Sonia with a flying tackle! The gun went off while the two of them were on their way to the floor, blasting a hole in the paneling. Sonia was flat out on her belly now, and I stepped on her wrist while Alex yanked the gun away from her.

Then we heard another loud sound, but this time from upstairs. I knew right away what it was: Dad had heard the blast and kicked in Mrs. Fields' door to see what was going on. "Get Dad down here!" I yelled to Mandy, and she went flying up the steps.

"Get off me, you big cow!" Sonia yelled, writhing around on the Astroturf carpet. Aggie responded by putting her in a full nelson wrestling hold.

CHAPTER TWELVE

The next morning my parents were seated in front of Mandy's laptop at the dining room table, engaged in a video chat with Alex and Aggie's mom. Ms. Burke cocked her head and narrowed her eyes as my parents shared details that became stranger by the second. The four of us twins stood stock-still behind my parents' chairs. We must have looked like we were in a police lineup. At least it sure felt that way.

"Let me get this straight," Ms. Burke interrupted. "They based all this on some images they think they saw in the wallpaper?"

"I know it sounds crazy, Mom," Aggie piped up. "But you've got to believe us."

"I just don't know what to believe anymore," Ms. Burke responded, shaking her head. "What is it with you four? I'm afraid that one of these days you'll get seriously hurt. Maybe even killed."

"We can't just ignore people when they need help," Alex said. "You're the one who taught us that. 'Follow the Golden Rule,' you always say."

Ms. Burke waved a hand in front of her face, obviously upset that Alex was trying to turn her words against her. "Well, from now on, if you think a dead person is contacting you for help, you have my permission to just say no." She said it seriously, but it sounded so funny that I couldn't help laughing. It started out as just a little snort, but when the other twins caught the bug as well, we all started cracking up.

My father turned toward us. "That's enough!" he thundered and stared us into absolute silence. He looked into the camera again. "See, Lori? They think this is all just some kind of game. For two summers in a row now they've managed to find themselves on the business end of some lunatic's gun."

"It's got to stop," my mother chimed in. "It'll just have to stop."

"We're all on the same page then," Ms. Burke assured her. "Maybe they just shouldn't get together anymore. Not even through the video chats."

"If that's what it takes to keep them safe," Mom agreed.

The four of us were wide-eyed. Over a thousand miles separated our homes, but it might as well be over a million if we were forbidden to see each other. My stomach clenched at the thought of not spending time with Aggie until we were eighteen, when our parents couldn't stop us anymore. I would even miss Alex. I respected him more than I liked him, but I would miss him too.

I fought the urge to cry out like a little kid, *That's not fair!* I knew that a tantrum would just cause the adults to hold their position more firmly. I swallowed hard and struggled to find the right words. "I'm really sorry I laughed," I began. "I'm sorry that we've caused you to worry. But keeping us totally apart just doesn't seem fair to me. The four of us are really good for each other. Mom and Dad, you always say you want Mandy and me to choose friends who bring out the best in us. Well, that's what the Burkes do. And I know all the supernatural stuff sounds really crazy. It does to me too. But we can't ignore it. Everybody in this world has different gifts, and maybe this is one that we were given. Please don't force us apart because of it. We all mean too much to each other." By the time I finished talking, my eyes were stinging.

"We don't *want* to force you apart," my mother said sincerely. "This is just about keeping you all safe."

"Okay, how about this?" Dad began and paused. "What if the kids promise to alert us if one of these . . . events occurs again? In other words, right away—before it goes too far."

I looked at the other three and they all nodded yes. We really didn't have a choice. "We could do that," I said for all of us. "I mean, we *promise* to do that."

"Lori?" Dad prompted Ms. Burke.

"I suppose I could live with that," she said. "And I'll do my best to keep an open mind."

"We all will," my mother added.

"Okay, it's a deal then," my father announced. "In the meantime, I need to take care of a little damage control to keep our kids' names out of the media." He turned to face us. "And remember, not a word about this to any of your friends. Got it?"

"Got it," we said in a chorus. My eyes met Aggie's, and both of us smiled.

****

I couldn't get to sleep that night. My parents had kept us in the house for the entire day, and all we did was watch movies and play games. Alex and I endured our two most boring chess matches ever because neither one of us was focused enough to mount an aggressive attack. Both ended in stalemate. Even Wii bowling, which I normally love, felt pretty blah. I wondered if Aunt Arabella had ever tried it.

Now my clock radio was showing 12:18 AM. That meant it was Sunday already and we would be driving the Burkes to Hopkins Airport in just eight hours. Alex was sound asleep on the bed, softly snoring with every third inhalation. I counted. I lay on the cot with my hands clasped behind my head, staring up at the ceiling fan in the dim moonlight. *How many times will it rotate between now and when we get in the car?* I wondered. I started to do crazy estimates in my head based on the number of rotations per minute. Then I suddenly stood up. I slipped on a pair of athletic shorts and tiptoed out of the room.

"Aggie?" I whispered at the foot of my sister's bed.

"I'm awake," she whispered back.

"Come on downstairs."

She quietly followed me to the family room, where I clicked on the floor lamp to its lowest level. Aggie was wearing an oversized Minnesota Lynx T-shirt that came down to her knees. Her hair was loose for the first time that week. It looked really pretty like that. We sat down next to each other on the couch and just remained in silence for a while. The whole scene felt dreamy to me— the soft lighting, the quiet of the room, my closeness to Aggie.

"You know, Sarah and I broke up," I finally said.

"To be honest with you, I kind of figured," she replied. "I mean, you haven't seen her since the basketball game."

"So . . . that's that."

"Why? I mean, why did you break up?"

"I guess it was my doing. For a couple of reasons. One, I was getting pretty fed up with how Barbie and bossy she can be." Then I just stared at Aggie.

"Okay, so what's the other reason?" she asked.

"You're the other reason," I finally said. "Us." I was nervous.

Aggie let out a long sigh and furrowed her brow. "And you wait until the very last day to tell me this? Why, Mark?"

"It's finally hitting me that I won't get to see you again until . . . who knows when?" And then I laid it on the line. "You're the most important girl in the world to me, Aggie. I wish I could have been honest with you—and with myself—right when you got here."

The silence was nearly unbearable. I felt like I was smothering inside a cocoon. And then Aggie leaned over and kissed me gently on the lips, breathing fresh life into me. "You're the most important boy to me, Mark," she said reluctantly, as if confessing to a teacher that she had forgotten to study for a major test.

"So, is that a problem or something?" I asked with a laugh.

"It is when *you* live in Ohio and *I* live in North Dakota," she replied seriously.

"We still have our video chats. And I'll talk my parents into letting Mandy and me come out your way at Christmas. And you could come back here next August for the Twins Days Festival." I was all puffed up with possibilities.

"Look, boyfriend-girlfriend relationships are hard enough when you live in the same town," Aggie said, deflating me. "You know that, Mark. How are we supposed to make it work across the country?"

"What are you saying then?" I asked. I was confused. It seemed like I was about to get dumped after Aggie and I were only a half-minute into our new relationship.

"We're just so young. We don't need to make the kind of commitment where—"

"Is there someone else you want to go out with?" I interrupted. I was jealous. "Is it that Rick guy you went to the dance with?"

She took both of my hands in hers. "No, it's nothing like that. I just don't want us getting into something, and then somebody winds up getting really hurt."

I flashed back to the parking lot at Wright-Patterson Air Force Base. I understood Aggie's fear of being hurt again, of being abandoned by someone who is supposed to love her and look out for her. I almost said, "I'm nothing like your father," but I managed to hold my tongue. A tear rolled down Aggie's cheek. "I understand," was all I said. I brushed the tear away and kissed her on the forehead.

"Thanks," she sniffled. "For now, let's leave it where we just found it: We're really important to each other. Let's leave it there and . . . Who knows? Maybe someday we'll be at the same college together or something."

"I'm willing to meet you halfway," I said, getting her to smile. "Somewhere in Wisconsin, I guess."

"Madison?"

"Madison works for me," I said. Aggie and I shook hands. My family and I had spent two nights in Madison the previous summer—one night on our way to North Dakota, and one on our way back home—and the place looked nice enough to me. "Even better yet," I continued, "maybe I can talk you into becoming a Buckeye at Ohio State. Great school."

"Nope. It's Madison," she teased. "We already shook on it." She stood up. "Come on. Let's get back to our beds before your father wakes up and decides to check window locks or something."

We held hands walking through the dining room and living room and even up the stairs. Just outside Mandy's bedroom door, Aggie and I held each other tight. I buried my face in the sweetness of her hair, knowing that this embrace would have to last me a long time. My parents' wind-up clock made its presence known, ticking us closer and closer to Aggie's departure. I didn't want to let go. I was numb with sadness at the thought of saying good-bye. But I was also confident that it wouldn't be our final farewell. Not by a long shot.

The End

SNEAK PEEK:
DOUBLE-TWINS MYSTERY #3

The Waikiki Witness

"Your father may be many things," Ms. Burke tells her twins, Alex and Aggie, "but a killer isn't one of them. I know that in my heart." The man in question has been charged with the murder of another sergeant while on assignment at Hickam Air Force Base in Hawaii.

As we already know, Alex and Aggie have an explosive relationship with their father since he divorced their mother years ago, abandoned the family, and quickly remarried. The twins eventually decide, however, that it is their duty to help the man. After all, they—along with the Cousineau twins—have an impressive record of solving the separate murders of Bobby Swenson and Arabella Hoffer.

The Burke twins are soon reunited with the Cousineaus, Mark and Mandy, for a trip to Hawaii. Join the Double-Twins on this tropical, mysterious adventure!

The Waikiki Witness, the final novel in the Double-Twins Mystery Series, is scheduled for release in 2017.

ABOUT THE AUTHOR

Paul Kijinski is the author of the novel *Camp Limestone*, winner of a 2007 Paterson Prize for Books for Young Readers, and other works of middle grade fiction. *The 11:15 Bench*, published in 2013, is a novel for adult readers.

Kijinski was born in Garfield Heights, Ohio, and earned degrees from Oberlin College, The Ohio State University, and John Carroll University. He began writing seriously while serving as a missile officer in the U.S. Air Force. The solitude of underground launch control centers provided a uniquely rich environment for putting pen to paper. His final assignment in the military was teaching English at the Air Force Academy.

Kijinski is currently an elementary school teacher in South Euclid, Ohio. He and his wife, Eileen, have two adult sons.

You may follow him on Facebook.